UNWIN HYMAN SH

SNAKES AND

LADDERS

INCLUDING
FOLLOW ON
ACTIVITIES

EDITED BY H. T. ROBERTSON

Published in 1988 by
Unwin Hyman Limited
15–17 Broadwick Street
London W1V 1FP

Reprinted 1990

British Library Cataloguing in Publication Data
Snakes and ladders.
  I. Robertson, H.T.
  823'.01'08 [FS]

  ISBN 0-04-448004-0

Typeset by TJB Photosetting Ltd., South Witham, Lincolnshire
Printed in Great Britain by Billing & Sons Ltd., Worcester

Series cover design by Iain Lanyon
Cover illustration by Alasdair Gray

Contents

Introduction

Welcome to this collection which reflects the work of a number of contemporary writers who reside in Scotland. Three writers have generously contributed personal reflections on their craft and their preoccupations: these are not, however, limited to their place of origin; indeed, they're universal.

But why Scotland? It is a 'nation' which is steeped in history but which has never found its soul. Scotland's distance from the perceived centre of culture and power has produced both a sense of alienation and a fervent desire for, and confusion about, a common identity. Now, as liberating materialism rolls back the frontiers of our society, the underclasses are gradually revealed, not only on flickering screens, but in the timeless words of those writers who have the humanity to recognize them – the children, the aged, the isolated, the deprived. Yet it's not all coldly depressing. Many of the stories reflect a wry humour and affirmation of life.

Why should teachers continue to present the short story, apparently flourishing but still read by few, to a generation of students whose interest is said to be as long as programme length or as brief as the most sensual advertisement? Image replaces thought: issues are reduced to images. Advertising *is* morality.

I have found in compiling this collection, a new and ruthless respect for the short story form. To paraphrase another writer, a novel is like a jumbo jet; it contains a cast of hundreds and can travel to the ends of the earth. A short story is like a balloon, containing few passengers, but it can ascend to undreamed-of heights. The stories here are more akin to long poems, more accessible but still superbly crafted. Pattern and form are paramount. Some mirror those for whom the centre has not held, but for whom – except perhaps one – anarchy is not an option. The protagonists ask for sympathy, acknowledgement of their existence. A bond is formed.

The selection and the follow on materials have been designed for students following courses in Standard Grade, GCSE, New Higher and Certificate of Sixth Year Studies, Scotvec courses, and should help them compile folios (assignments) of their own creative/discursive writing and personal/imaginative responses to literature, as well as fostering the meeting of minds during discussion.

Some of the 'Before Reading' activities are intended to form a context, a personal frame of reference for the student within which to place the stories. Thus personal experience may be enriched and enlightened by that of others. Teachers are therefore recommended to preview these materials before introducing the stories, and to read Brian McCabe's 'Kreativ Riting' before proceeding any further.

H.T. Robertson

JOAN LINGARD

Silver Linings

Every cloud is supposed to have one, or so I learned at my granny's knee. Isn't that where you're supposed to learn such things? My granny is full of sayings, most of them rubbish, according to my mother, who has her own sayings. Like most mothers. My granny isn't one of those grandmothers who sits and knits in the chimney corner, shrouded in shawls, if such grannies exist at all. She tints her hair auburn and is employed as manageress at a local supermarket. It's not all that 'super', I must add, as it's only got two aisles, one up and one down, but still, a job's a job these days. And money doesn't grow ...

Money's a problem in our family and my granny helps keep us afloat with 'care' parcels. She dumps them down on the kitchen table muttering about the improvidence of my parents and the wasted education of my mother who had all the chances in life that she didn't have herself. Etcetera. My father is not a lot of use when it comes to providing. He does odd jobs and he comes and goes. Like driftwood, says my granny, who doesn't understand what her daughter saw in him.

I think it was probably his name. He's called Torquil. My mother's got a thing about names. Her own given name was Isobel. A good plain no-nonsense Scottish Christian name. The only person who uses it now is my granny. My mother is known to everyone else as Isabella or Bella.

My name is Samantha, which my mother uses in full, but

my friends call me Sam and my brother's called Seb, short for Sebastian. My granny approves of neither the short nor the long versions. 'Sam and Seb – sounds like two cartoon characters!' She hates having to introduce us, it gives her a 'red face'. She had wanted us to be called Jean and Colin. So she calls me hen and Seb, son.

Anyway, to get back to silver linings. I don't know about clouds having them but for a short time we had in our possession a fur coat which had one. But, first, I'd better explain about my mother's shop.

She keeps a second-hand clothes shop in a street that's full of shops selling second-hand things, from books to old fenders and clocks to medals and feather boas (though they're scarce) and silk petticoats (usually full of snaps and runs) and woollens (usually washed in). There are also two or three bars in the street, and some cafés. We like it, Seb and I. There's always something going on. The shop's in a basement (a damp one) across the road from our flat. You can doubtless imagine what my granny thinks of it. She says the smell of the old clothes turns her stomach and folk that buy stuff like that need their heads examined.

But people do come in and buy, not that it's ever like the shops in Princes Street on a Saturday. And they tend to sit on boxes and blether to my mother for hours before they get round to buying some ghastly looking dress with a V neck and a drooping hemline that was fasionable during the war. And then they find they haven't got quite enough money to pay for it so my mother says she'll get it from them the next time they're in. You can see why we need the care parcels.

When my mother goes out on the rummage for new stock – new old stock, that is – she just shuts up the shop and leaves a note on the door saying 'Back in ten minutes' or, if I'm home from school, she leaves me in charge with my friend Morag. (Nice name, Morag, says my granny.) Morag and I amuse ourselves by trying on the clothes and parading up and down like models. We usually have a good laugh too. I like long traily dresses in black crêpe de chine and big floppy hats and Morag likes silks and satins. We don't bother with the washed-in woollies.

One day my mother came back in a taxi filled to bursting with old clothes. She was bursting with excitement too, even gave the taxi driver a pound tip. You'd have thought we were about to make our fortune!

Morag and I helped to haul in the catch. We sat on the floor in the middle of it and unpacked the bags. There were dresses of every colour of the rainbow, made of silk and of satin, of brocade and of very fine wool.

'They belonged to an old lady,' said my mother.

The dresses smelt really old when you pressed them to your face.

'She died last month.'

We shivered a little and let the dresses fall into our laps.

'She was *very* old though.'

We cheered up and turned our attention to the blouses and scarves and the satin shoes. The old lady must never have thrown anything away.

And then out of a bag I took a fur coat. Now my mother doesn't like fur coats, usually won't handle them. By that, I mean sell them. She's for Beauty Without Cruelty. As I am myself. But this coat felt kind of smooth and silky, even though it was a bit bald looking here and there, and so I slipped it on.

'I'll have to get rid of that quickly,' said my mother.

I stroked the fur.

'Poor animal,' said my mother.

I slipped my hands into the pockets. I was beginning to think there was something funny about the coat. The lining felt odd, sort of lumpy, and I thought I could hear a faint rustling noise coming from inside it. I took the coat off.

The lining had been mended in a number of places by someone who could sew very fine stitches. I lifted the scissors and quickly began to snip the thread.

'What are you doing that for?' asked my mother irritably.

'Wait!'

I eased my hand up between the lining and the inside of the coat and brought out a five pound note. Morag gasped. And then I brought out another and another and then a ten pound one and then another five and a ten –

'I don't believe it!' said my mother, who looked as pale as the off-white blouse she was crumpling between her hands.

We extracted from the lining of the coat one thousand and ten pounds in old bank notes. They were creased and aged, but they were real enough. We sat in silence and stared at them. My mother picked up a ten pound note and peered at it in the waning afternoon light.

'She can't have trusted the bank. Old people are sometimes funny that way. Keep their money in mattresses and places.' Like old coats.

'We could go for a holiday,' I said.

'A Greek island,' murmured my mother. 'Paros. Or Naxos.'

Once upon a time she used to wander around islands, with my father, before Seb and I were born. I could see us, the three of us, lying on the warm sand listening to the soft swish of the blue blue sea.

'Are you going to keep it?' asked Morag, breaking into our trance. She's a bit like that, Morag, down-to-earth, a state of being that my granny is fully in favour of.

My mother bit the side of her lip, the way she does when she's a bit confused. She quite often bites her lip.

'Finder's keepers,' I said hopefully. Hadn't my granny taught me that?

'I did *pay* for the coat.'

Not a thousand pounds of course, we knew that.

'Who did you buy it from?' asked Morag.

'A relative of the old lady's. He was clearing out the house. He looked well enough heeled.'

'In that case –' I said.

'I'll need to think about it,' said my mother. 'In the meantime –' She glanced about her and I got up to put on the light and draw the curtains.

What *were* we to do with the money?

'We could sew it back into the coat,' I suggested.

That seemed as good an idea as any other so Morag and I pushed the notes back into the lining, all but one ten pound one which my mother said we might as well keep out to buy something for supper with that evening.

'Morag,' she said, sounding a bit awkward, 'don't be saying

anything about this to anyone else eh?'

'I wouldn't dream of it, Isabella.' (My mother likes my friends to call her by her Christian name. She likes Seb and me to do it too but when I'm talking about her I always refer to her as 'my mother'.)

When I chummed Morag along the street on her way home I told her I'd kill her if she did tell and we almost quarrelled as she said I'd no business to doubt her word. But it was such a big secret to keep! I felt choked up with the excitement of it.

We took the fur coat across the road with us when we went home and over an Indian carry-out and a bottle of rosé wine my mother and Seb and I discussed the problem of whether we were entitled to keep the money or not. Seb and I thought there was no problem at all.

'You bought the coat, Bella,' said Seb. 'Everything in it's yours.'

'Well, I don't know. Maybe, legally, but morally … I mean, I suppose I *should* give it back.'

'But you want to go to Greece don't you?' I said.

Her lip trembled.

Outside, it was raining. Big heavy drops were striking the window pane and the wind was making the glass rattle in its frame.

'You could both be doing with new shoes,' said our mother. 'Mind you, with money like that …' She sighed.

The next day was Saturday. We took the coat back over to the shop with us in the morning, afraid to let it out of our sight. My mother put it in a cupboard in the back room where she keeps garments that are waiting to be mended. Some are beyond redemption but they wait nevertheless.

In the afternoon, we had to go to a family wedding, on my father's side. My father was supposed to be there. My mother and I kitted ourselves out with clothes from the shop.

'Well, honestly!' declared my granny, on her arrival. She was to mind the shop while we were gone. 'I could have lent you a nice wee suit, Isobel.' She turned to look me over. 'Do you think black crêpe de chine's the right thing to be wearing at a wedding? And at your age too!' She didn't even call me hen. She couldn't have thought I looked endearing. The dress had come out of the old lady's wardrobe.

In the bus, Seb said to our mother, 'Now don't tell Father about the money if he *is* there.'

He did turn up. He was his usual 'charming' self, never stuck for words. I was pleased enough to see him to begin with but after a bit when I saw him sweet-talking our mother and her cheeks beginning to turn pink and her eyes lighting up, I felt myself going off him. Seb and I sat side by side and drank as much fizzy wine as we could get hold of and listened to her laugh floating down the room.

'She'll tell him,' said Seb gloomily.

She did of course. And he decided to come home with us. They walked in front of us holding hands.

'When will she ever learn?' said Seb, sounding strangely like our granny.

'Good evening, Torquil,' said that lady very stiffly, when we came into the shop where she was sitting playing Clock Patience on the counter top. 'Stranger,' she couldn't resist adding.

'Hi, Ma!' He gave her a smacking kiss on the cheek. 'It's good to see you. You're not looking a day older.'

She did not return the compliment.

'Been busy?' asked my mother.

'Not exactly rushed off my feet. I sold two or three dresses and one of those tatty Victorian nightgowns – oh, and yon moth-eaten fur coat in the cupboard through the back.'

She might just as well have struck us all down with a sledgehammer. We were in a state of total collapse for at least five minutes until my mother managed to get back the use of her tongue.

'You sold *that coat*?'

'Well, why not? You hate having fur lying around.'

'Who did you sell it to?' My mother was doing her best to stay calm.

'How should I know? Some woman. She came in asking if we'd any furs. She gave me twenty pounds for it. I didn't think you could ask a penny more. Lucky to get that.'

My mother told my granny about the money in the lining and then it was her turn to collapse. I thought we were going to have to call a doctor to revive her. My father managed it with some brandy that he had in his coat pocket.

'Oh no,' she moaned, 'oh *no*. But what did you leave it in the shop for, Isobel?'

'It was in the back shop! In the cupboard.'

They started to argue, to blame one another. Seb and I went out and roamed the streets till dark and long after looking for the woman in our fur coat. We never did see it again.

Our father left the next morning.

'Shows him up for what he is, doesn't it?' said our granny. 'He only came back for the money. He'd have taken you to the cleaners, Isobel. Maybe it was just as well. As I always say –' She stopped.

Not even she had the nerve to look my mother in the eye and say that every cloud has its silver lining.

A
BERNARD MACLAVERTY
Time To Dance

Nelson, with a patch over one eye, stood looking idly into Mothercare's window. The sun was bright behind him and made a mirror out of the glass. He looked at his patch with distaste and felt it with his finger. The elastoplast was rough and dry and he disliked the feel of it. Bracing himself for the pain, he ripped it off and let a yell out of him. A woman looked down at him curiously to see why he had made the noise but by that time he had the patch in his pocket. He knew without looking that some of his eyebrow would be on it.

He had spent most of the morning in the Gardens avoiding distant uniforms but now that it was coming up to lunchtime he braved it on to the street. He had kept his patch on longer than usual because his mother had told him the night before that if he didn't wear it he would go 'stark, staring blind'.

Nelson was worried because he knew what it was like to be blind. The doctor at the eye clinic had given him a box of patches that would last for most of his lifetime. Opticludes. One day Nelson had worn two and tried to get to the end of the street and back. It was a terrible feeling. He had to hold his head back in case it bumped into anything and keep waving his hands in front of him backwards and forwards like windscreen wipers. He kept tramping on tin cans and heard them trundle emptily away. Broken glass crackled under his feet and he could not figure out how close to the wall he was.

Several times he heard footsteps approaching, slowing down as if they were going to attack him in his helplessness, then walking away. One of the footsteps even laughed. Then he heard a voice he knew only too well.

'Jesus, Nelson, what are you up to this time?' It was his mother. She led him back to the house with her voice blaring in his ear.

She was always shouting. Last night, for instance, she had started into him for watching TV from the side. She had dragged him round to the chair in front of it.

'That's the way the manufacturers make the sets. They put the picture on the front. But oh no, that's not good enough for our Nelson. He has to watch it from the side. Squint, my arse, you'll just go blind – stark, staring blind.'

Nelson then had turned his head and watched it from the front. She had never mentioned the blindness before. Up until now all she had said was 'If you don't wear them patches that eye of yours will turn in till it's looking at your brains. God knows, not that it'll have much to look at.'

His mother was Irish. That was why she had a name like Skelly. That was why she talked funny. But she was proud of the way she talked and nothing angered her more than to hear Nelson saying 'Ah ken' and 'What like is it?' She kept telling him that someday they were going back when she had enough ha'pence scraped together. 'Until then I'll not let them make a Scotchman out of you.' But Nelson talked the way he talked.

His mother had called him Nelson because she said she thought that his father had been a seafaring man. The day the boy was born she had read an article in the *Reader's Digest* about Nelson Rockefeller, one of the richest men in the world. It seemed only right to give the boy a good start. She thought it also had the advantage that it couldn't be shortened, but she was wrong. Most of the boys in the scheme called him Nelly Skelly.

He wondered if he should sneak back to school for dinner then skive off again in the afternoon. They had good dinners at school – like a hotel, with choices. Chips and magic things like rhubarb crumble. There was one big dinner-woman who gave him extra every time she saw him. She told him he needed fattening. The only draw back to the whole system was that he was on free dinners. Other people in his class were given their dinner money and it was up to them whether they went without a dinner and bought Coke and sweets and stuff with the money. It was a choice Nelson didn't have, so he had to invent other things to get the money out of his mother. In Lent there was the Black Babies; library fines were worth the odd 10p although, as yet, he had not taken a book from the school library – and anyway they didn't have to pay fines, even if they were late; the Home Economics Department asked them to bring in money to buy their ingredients and Nelson would always add 20p to it.

'What the hell are they teaching you to cook – sides of beef?' his mother would yell. Outdoor pursuits required extra money. But even though they had ended after the second term Nelson went on asking for the 50p on a Friday – 'to go horse-riding'. His mother would never part with money without a speech of some sort.

'Horse riding? Horse riding! Jesus, I don't know what sort of a school I've sent you to. Is Princess Anne in your class or something? Holy God, horse riding.'

Outdoor pursuits was mostly walking round museums on wet days and, when it was dry, the occasional trip to Portobello beach to write on a flapping piece of foolscap the signs of pollution you could see. Nelson felt that the best outdoor pursuit of the lot was what he was doing now. Skiving. At least that way, you could do what you liked.

He groped into his pocket for the change out of his 50p and went into a shop. He bought a giant thing of bubblegum and crammed it into his mouth. It was hard and dry at first and he couldn't answer the woman when she spoke to him.

'Whaaungh?'

'Pick the paper off the floor, son! Use the basket.'

He picked the paper up and screwed in into a ball. He aimed to miss the basket, just to spite her, but it went in. By the time he reached the bottom of the street the gum was chewy. He thrust his tongue into the middle of it and blew. A small disappointing bubble burst with a plip. It was not until the far end of Princes Street that he managed to blow big ones, pink and wobbling, that he could see at the end of his nose which burst well and had to be gathered in shreds from his chin.

Then suddenly the crowds of shoppers parted and he saw his mother. In the same instant she saw him. She was on him before he could even think of running. She grabbed him by the fur of his parka jacket and began screaming into his face.

'In the name of God Nelson what are you doing here? Why aren't you at school?' She began shaking him. 'Do you realize what this means? They'll put me in bloody jail. It'll be bloody Saughton for me, and no mistake.' She had her teeth gritted together and her mouth was slanting in her face. Then Nelson started to shout.

'Help! Help!' he yelled.

A woman with an enormous chest like a pigeon stopped. 'What's happening?' she said.

Nelson's mother turned on her. 'It's none of your bloody business.'

'I'm being kidnapped,' yelled Nelson.

'Young woman. Young woman ...' said the lady with the large chest trying to tap Nelson's mother on the shoulder with her umbrella, but Mrs Skelly turned with such a snarl that the woman edged away hesitatingly and looked over her shoulder and tut-tutted just loudly enough for the passing crowd to hear her.

'Help! I'm being kidnapped,' screamed Nelson, but everybody walked past looking the other way. His mother squatted down in front of him, still holding on to his jacket. She lowered her voice and tried to make it sound reasonable.

'Look Nelson, love. Listen. If you're skiving school do you realize what'll happen to me? In Primary the Children's Panel threatened to send me to court. You're only at that Secondary and already that Sub-Attendance Committee thing wanted to fine me. Jesus if you're caught again ...'

Nelson stopped struggling. The change in her tone had quietened him down. She straightened up and looked wildly about her, wondering what to do.

'You've got to go straight back to school, do you hear me?'

'Yes.'

'Promise me you'll go.' The boy looked down at the ground.

11

'Promise?' The boy made no answer.

'I'll kill you if you don't go back. I'd take you myself only I've my work to go to. I'm late as it is.'

Again she looked around as if she would see someone who would suddenly help her. Still she held on to his jacket. She was biting her lip.

'O God, Nelson.'

The boy blew a flesh-pink bubble and snapped it between his teeth. She shook him.

'That bloody bubblegum.'

There was a loud explosion as the one o'clock gun went off. They both leapt.

'O Jesus, that gun puts the heart sideways in me everytime it goes off. Come on son, you'll have to come with me. I'm late. I don't know what they'll say when they see you but I'm bloody taking you to school by the ear. You hear me?'

She began rushing along the street, Nelson's sleeve in one hand, her carrier bag in the other. The boy had to run to keep from being dragged.

'Don't you dare try a trick like that again. Kidnapped, my arse. Nelson if I knew somebody who would kidnap you I'd pay HIM the money. Embarrassing me on the street like that.'

They turned off the main road and went into a hallway and up carpeted stairs which had full-length mirrors along one side. Nelson stopped to make faces at himself but his mother chugged at his arm. At the head of the stairs stood a fat man in his shirtsleeves.

'What the hell is this?' he said. 'You're late, and what the hell is that?' He looked down from over his stomach at Nelson.

'I'll explain later,' she said. 'I'll let him stay in the room.'

'You should be on NOW,' he said and turned and walked away through the swing doors. They followed him and Nelson saw, before his mother pushed him into the room, that it was a bar, plush and carpeted with crowds of men standing drinking.

'You sit here Nelson until I'm finished and then I'm taking you back to that school. You'll get nowhere if you don't do your lessons. I have to get changed now.'

She set her carrier bag on the floor and kicked off her shoes.

Nelson sat down watching her. She stopped and looked over her shoulder at him, biting her lip.

'Where's that bloody eyepatch you should be wearing?' Nelson indicated his pocket.

'Well wear it then.' Nelson took the crumpled patch from his pocket, tugging bits of it unstuck to get it flat before he stuck it over his bad eye. His mother took out her handbag and began rooting about at the bottom of it. Nelson heard the rattle of her bottles of scent and tubes of lipstick.

'Ah,' she said and produced another eyepatch, flicking it clean. 'Put another one on till I get changed. I don't want you noseying at me.' She came to him pulling away the white backing to the patch and stuck it over his remaining eye. He imagined that the tip of her tongue was stuck out, concentrating. When she spooned medicine into him *she* opened her mouth as well. She pressured his eyebrows with her thumbs, making sure that the patches were stuck.

'Now don't move or you'll bump into something.'

Nelson heard the slither of her clothes and her small grunts as she hurriedly got changed. Then he heard her rustle in her bag, the soft pop and rattle as she opened her capsules. Her 'tantalizers' she called them, small black and red torpedoes. Then he heard her voice.

'Just you stay like that till I come back. That way you'll come to no harm. You hear me Nelson? If I come back in here and you have those things off, I'll KILL you. I'll not be long.'

Nelson nodded from his darkness.

'The door will be locked so there's no running away.'

'Ah ken.'

Suddenly his darkness exploded with lights as he felt her bony hand strike his ear.

'You don't ken things, Nelson. You *know* them.'

He heard her go out and the key turn in the lock. His ear sang and he felt it was hot. He turned his face up to the ceiling. She had left the light on because he could see pinkish through the patches. He smelt the beer and stale smoke. Outside the room pop music had started up, very loudly. He heard the deep notes pound through to where he sat. He felt his ear with his hand and it *was* hot.

Making small aww sounds of excruciating pain, he slowly detached both eye-patches from the bridge of his nose outwards. In case his mother should come back he did not take them off completely, but left them hinged to the sides of his eyes. When he turned to look around him they flapped like blinkers.

It wasn't really a room, more a broom cupboard. Crates were stacked against one wall; brushes and mops and buckets stood near a very low sink; on a row of coathooks hung some limp raincoats and stained white jackets; his mother's stuff hung on the last hook. The floor was covered with tramped flat cork tips. Nelson got up to look at what he was sitting on. It was a crate of empties. He went to the keyhole and looked out but all he could see was a patch of wallpaper opposite. Above the door was a narrow window. He looked up at it, his eye patches falling back to touch his ears. He went over to the sink and had a drink of water from the low tap, sucking in noisily at the column of water as it splashed into the sink. He stopped and wiped his mouth. The water felt cold after the mint of the bubblegum. He looked up at his mother's things, hanging on the hook; her tights and drawers were as she wore them but inside out and hanging knock-kneed on top of everything. In her bag he found her blonde wig and tried it on, smelling the perfume of it as he did so. At home he liked noseying in his mother's room; smelling all her bottles of make-up; seeing her spangled things. He had to stand on the crate to see himself but the mirror was all brown measles under its surface and the eye-patches ruined the effect. He sat down again and began pulling at his bubblegum, seeing how long he could make it stretch before it broke. Still the music pounded outside. It was so loud the vibrations tickled his feet. He sighed and looked up at the window again.

If his mother took him back to school he could see problems. For starting St John the Baptist's she had bought him a brand new Adidas bag for his books. Over five pounds it had cost her, she said. On his first real skive he had dumped the bag in the bin at the bottom of his stair, every morning for a week, and travelled light into town. On the Friday he came home just in time to see the bin lorry driving away in a cloud of bluish smoke. He had told his mother that the bag had been stolen from the playground during break. She had threatened to phone the school about it but Nelson had hastily assured her that the whole matter was being investigated by none other than the Headmaster himself. This threat put the notion out of his head of asking her for the money to replace the books. At that point he had not decided on a figure. He could maybe try it again sometime when all the fuss had died down. But now it was all going to be stirred if his mother took him to school.

He pulled two crates to the door and climbed up but it was not high enough. He put a third one on top and gingerly straightened, balancing on its rim. On tip-toe he could see out. He couldn't see his mother anywhere. He saw a crowd of men standing in a semi-circle. Behind them were some very bright lights, red, yellow and blue. They all had pints in their hands which they didn't seem to be drinking. They were all watching something which Nelson couldn't see. Suddenly the music stopped and the men all began drinking and talking. Standing on tip-toe for so long, Nelson's legs began to shake and he heard the bottles in the crate rattle. He rested for a moment. Then the music started again. He looked to see. The men now just stood looking. It was as if they were seeing a ghost. Then they all cheered louder than the music.

Nelson climbed down and put the crates away from the door so that his mother could get in. He closed his eye-patches over for a while but still she didn't come. He listened to another record, this time a slow one. He decided to travel blind to get another drink of water. As he did so the music changed to fast. He heard the men cheering again, then the rattle of the key in the lock. Nelson, his arms rotating in front of him, tried to make his way back to the crate. His mother's voice said,

'Don't you dare take those eye-patches off.' Her voice was panting. Then his hand hit up against her. It was her bare stomach, hot and damp with sweat. She guided him to sit down, breathing heavily through her nose.

'I'll just get changed and then you're for school right away, boy.' Nelson nodded. He heard her light a cigarette as she dressed. When she had finished she ripped off his right eye-patch.

'There now, we're ready to go,' she said, ignoring Nelson's anguished yells.

'That's the wrong eye,' he said.

'Oh shit,' said his mother and ripped off the other one, turned it upside down and stuck it over his right eye. The smoke from the cigarette in her mouth trickled up into her eye and she held it half shut. Nelson could see the bright points of sweat shining through her make-up. She sill hadn't got her breath back fully yet. She smelt of drink.

On the way out the fat man with the rolled up sleeves held out two fivers and Nelson's mother put them into her purse.

'The boy – never again,' he said, looking down at Nelson.

They took the number twelve to St John the Baptist's. It was the worst possible time because, just as they were going in, the bell rang for the end of a period and suddenly the quad was full of pupils, all looking at Nelson and his mother. Some sixth-year boys wolf-whistled after her and others stopped to stare. Nelson felt a flush of pride that she was causing a stir. She was dressed in black satiny jeans, very tight, and her pink blouse was knotted, leaving her tanned midriff bare. They went into the office and a secretary came to the window.

'Yes?' she said, looking Mrs Skelly up and down.

'I'd like to see the Head,' she said.

'I'm afraid he's at a meeting. What is it about?'

'About him.' She waved her thumb over her shoulder at Nelson.

'What year is he?'

'What year are you, son?' His mother turned to him.

'First.'

'First Year. Oh then you'd best see Mr Mac Dermot, the First Year Housemaster.' The secretary directed them to Mr Mac Dermot's office. It was at the other side of the school and they had to walk what seemed miles of corridors before they found it. Mrs Skelly's stiletto heels clicked along the tiles.

'It's a wonder you don't get lost in here, son,' she said as she knocked on the Housemaster's door. Mr Mac Dermot opened it and invited them in. Nelson could see that he, too was looking at her, his eyes wide and his face smiley.

'What can I do for you?' he said when they were seated.

'It's him,' said Mrs Skelly. 'He's been skiving again. I caught him this morning.'

'I see,' said Mr Mac Dermot. He was very young to be a Housemaster. He had a black moustache which he began to stroke with the back of his hand. He paused for a long time. Then he said,

'Remind me of your name, son.'

'– Oh I'm sorry,' said Mrs Skelly. 'My name is Skelly and this is my boy Nelson.'

'Ah yes Skelly.' The Housemaster got up and produced a yellow file from the filing cabinet. 'You must forgive me but we haven't seen a great deal of Nelson lately.'

'Do you mind if I smoke?' asked Mrs Skelly.

'Not at all,' said the Housemaster, getting up to open the window.

'The trouble is, that the last time we were at that Sub-attendance committee thing they said they would take court action if it happened again. And it has.'

'Well it may not come to that with the Attendance Sub-Committee. If we nip it in the bud. If Nelson makes an effort, isn't that right Nelson?' Nelson sat silent.

'Speak when the master's speaking to you,' yelled Mrs Skelly.

'Yes,' said Nelson, making it just barely audible.

'You're Irish too,' said Mrs Skelly to the Housemaster, smiling.

'That's right,' said Mr Mac Dermot. 'I thought your accent was familiar. Where do you come from?'

'My family come from just outside Derry. And you?'

'Oh that's funny. I'm just across the border from you. Donegal.' As they talked Nelson stared out the window. He had never heard his mother so polite. He could just see a corner of the playing fields and a class coming out with the Gym teacher. Nelson hated Gym more than anything. It was crap. He loathed the changing rooms, the getting stripped in front of others, the stupidity he felt when he missed the ball. The smoke from his mother's cigarette went in an arc towards the open window. Distantly he could hear the class shouting as they started a game of football.

'Nelson! Isn't that right?' said Mr Mac Dermot loudly.

'What?'

'That even when you are here you don't work hard enough.'

'Hmm,' said Nelson.

'You don't have to tell me,' said his mother. 'It's not just his eye that's lazy. If you ask me the whole bloody lot of him is. I've never seen him washing a dish in his life and he leaves everything at his backside.'

'Yes,' said the Housemaster. Again he stroked his moustache. 'What is required from Nelson is a change of attitude. Attitude, Nelson. You understand a word like attitude?'

'Yes.'

'He's just not interested in school, Mrs Skelly.'

'I've no room to talk, of course. I had to leave at fifteen,' she said rolling her eyes in Nelson's direction. 'You know what I mean? Otherwise I might have stayed on and got my exams.'

'I see,' said Mr Mac Dermot. 'Can we look forward to a change in attitude, Nelson?'

'Hm-hm.'

'Have you no friends in school?' asked the Housemaster.

'Naw.'

'And no interest. You see you can't be interested in any subject unless you do some work at it. Work pays dividends with interest ...' he paused and looked at Mrs Skelly. She was inhaling her cigarette. He went on, 'Have you considered the possibility that Nelson may be suffering from school phobia?'

Mrs Skelly looked at him. 'Phobia, my arse,' she said. 'He just doesn't like school.'

'I see. Does he do any work at home then?'

'Not since he had his bag with all his books in it stolen.'

'Stolen?'

Nelson leaned forward in his chair and said loudly and clearly, 'I'm going to try to be better from now on. I am. I am going to try, sir.'

'That's more like it,' said the Housemaster, also edging forward.

'I am not going to skive. I am going to try. Sir, I'm going to do my best.'

18

'Good boy. I think Mrs Skelly if I have a word with the right people and convey to them what we have spoken about, I think there will be no court action. Leave it with me, will you? And I'll see what I can do. Of course it all depends on Nelson. If he is as good as his word. One more truancy and I'll be forced to report it. And he must realize that he has three full years of school to do before he leaves us. You must be aware of my position in this matter. You understand what I'm saying, Nelson?'

'Ah ken,' he said. 'I know.'

'You go off to your class now. I have some more things to say to your mother.'

Nelson rose to his feet and shuffled towards the door. He stopped.

'Where do I go, sir?'

'Have you not got your time-table?'

'No sir. Lost it.'

The Housemaster, tut-tutting, dipped into another file, read a card and told him that he should be at R.K. in Room 72. As he left Nelson noticed that his mother had put her knee up against the Housemaster's desk and was swaying back in her chair, as she took out another cigarette.

'Bye love,' she said.

When he went into Room 72 there was a noise of oo's and ahh's from the others in the class. He said to the teacher that he had been seeing Mr Mac Dermot. She gave him a Bible and told him to sit down. He didn't know her name. He had her for English as well as R.K. She was always rabbiting on about poetry.

'You boy, that just came in. For your benefit we are talking and reading about organization. Page 667. About how we should divide our lives up with work and prayer. How we should put each part of the day to use, and each part of the year. This is one of the most beautiful passages in the whole of the Bible. Listen to its rhythms as I read.' She lightly drummed her closed fist on the desk in front of her.

' "There is an appointed time for everything, and a time for every affair under the heavens. A time to be born and a time to die; a time to plant and a time to uproot..." '

'What page did you say Miss?' asked Nelson.

'Six-six-seven,' she snapped and read on, her voice trembling. ' "A time to kill and a time to heal; a time to wear down and a time to build. A time to weep and a time to laugh; a time to mourn and a time to dance..." '

Nelson looked out of the window, at the tiny white H of the goalposts in the distance. He took his bubblegum out and stuck it under the desk. The muscles of his jaw ached from chewing the now flavourless mass. He looked down at page 667 with its microscopic print, then put his face close to it. He tore off his eye-patch thinking that if he was going to become blind then the sooner it happened the better.

BRIAN McCABE

*A*nima

'Hurry up and make up yer mind,' said my father.

I went on staring at the dinette linoleum in silence. It wasn't yellow and it wasn't quite brown, but a sort of diarrhoea-colour in between. It was making me feel queasy, staring at it like this. I remembered my sister telling me that its pattern was called *parquet* and that it was just like Mum to buy lino that pretended to be wood. What had she meant by that? And what had she meant when she'd said that a dinette wasn't the same thing as a dining room? What was the difference? And why did we call it the dinette anyway? Nobody ate in here. Everybody ate in the living room, with the telly on and the fire. The only thing anyone ever did in the dinette was sulk. That was what it was for.

'Come *on*,' moaned my father, 'decide what to be and geez peace!'

What to be. How could I decide what to be? It had been hard enough deciding to join the cubs. Now this: what to *be*? It was cold in the dinette, but I felt strangely hot inside – hot and shivery. I pretended to look out of the window at the garden, hoping my father would go away. Then I found myself looking out at it – at the weeds and the old gas cooker and the hut made of railway sleepers. It was getting dark, and the hut looked like a little animal cowering against the wall. I noticed the packet of seeds on the windowsill, picked it up and pretended to be reading the instructions. I'd bought the seeds weeks ago and my father had promised to show me how to plant them. He'd forgotten about it though. I heard him making the most of a yawn – why did he always do that? – and I knew that he was fed up with this father-and-son routine in the dinette. He wanted to be in the living room, watching the news and arguing with the Prime Minister. Instead he'd been sent in to talk to me because I was sulking.

I glanced up at him as he yawned again. He stood just inside the door, slouched forwards like a tired old bull. His belly hung over the sagging waistband of his trousers and his braces hung loose. His trousers and shirt were unbuttoned and his vest was a greyish colour. I started shaking the packet to hear the seeds. It sounded like they were whispering to each other in there.

'Come *on*. Ah've no got aa night!'

I looked at his face to see if the anger in his voice was real or just pretend. He stuck his head forward and glowered down at me in mockery, mimicking my own frown. Why wasn't he young, like other people's dads, and interested in hunting and fishing and camping and cars? Or at least in gardening? Why did my dad have to be old and tired, with thick tufts of hair sticking out of his nostrils and his ears? All he was interested in was politics and horse-racing and going to the pub. Why had my mother sent him in to talk to me? How could he help me to decide what to be? He didn't even know what it was like to be a cub.

'D'ye want to be a frogman, or what?'

That was typical. How could I be a frogman? I didn't have flippers, I didn't have goggles. Maybe the snorkel and the rubber suit could be pretended, but that wasn't enough.

I shook my head, stared at the lino and felt ill.

'How about an astronaut, then?' This time I shook my head even before I let myself begin to imagine the impossible silver suit, the helmet and the window in the front... 'Why no? Like Yuri Gagarin, eh?'

'How can I?' I heard my own voice whine, 'Astronauts've got silver suits and ... and I don't!'

'Oh ho ho,' said my father, 'oh ho ho ho ho ...' He went on

ho-hoing until it sounded almost like a real laugh, then he coughed and spluttered. 'Well, ye'll just have to be a wee monkey then, eh? That shouldnae be too hard!'

That was typical as well. All he could do was mock. He didn't understand how important it all was. As he opened the door to go out, he turned and made a face as if he was going to say something serious, which meant he was going to make a joke.

'Ach well,' he said, 'ye'll just have to go as yersel. One of the lumpen proletariat.'

What did that mean? What was the proletariat, and what had happened to its leg? As my father shut the door I threw the packet of seeds on the floor. It burst open and the tiny seeds scattered over the linoleum. They looked like insects running away when their stone has been lifted. I saw my own shadow on the floor and suddenly it looked like a giant's shadow and the hot-shivery feeling swept over me again. No, I wasn't going to be ill. If I admitted feeling ill, they wouldn't let me go at all.

I crossed the room and looked at myself in the mirror above the sideboard. Maybe I could be a pirate? But no, too many of the others would go as pirates, and their pirates would have eye-patches and cutlasses and bright, spotted neckerchiefs. My pirate would have a soot-blackened face and an old headscarf round his neck and that would be it. Too much like a real pirate, maybe. Or a cowboy? But no, somehow that was too obvious. I needed to think of something better to be, something original.

'What a fuss to make about a party,' said my sister as she came into the room. She came towards me then stood with her arms folded, staring at me. 'Right,' she said, 'you'll never get anywhere or be anybody if you can't decide what to go as to a stupid fancy-dress party at the cubs. Turn round.'

I obeyed slowly, then stared at her elbows. This meant that I could avoid her eyes, which were too honest to look at for long without feeling guilty, and her breasts, which were too much a source of fascination and confusion.

'A pirate,' she said. I mumbled something about cutlasses and ear-rings. 'Chinaman,' she stated. I hesitated. Was it possible to be a Chinaman?

'But how could I make my eyes like a Chinaman's?' I whined, but my sister was already grasping me by both shoulders and turning me this way and that, looking me up and down, as if she could somehow tell whether or not I had the makings of a half-decent Chinaman in me.

'I'd have to use a curtain for the robe,' said my sister, 'a lampshade for your hat and ... make-up for the eyes...' Suddenly she stopped turning me and held me still and I felt the queasy feeling again – as if I'd jumped off a spinning roundabout. '*I* know what you should be!' She took a step back and clapped her hands.

'What?' I said, beginning to feel wary.

'A girl.'

A girl! Was she out of her mind? I opened my mouth to speak, but my sister got there first:

'You can wear one of my old skirts. The pink one with the zip at the back ... We'll have to get you some stockings and high-heels – I'll teach you how to walk in them, it isn't easy – and that blouse, that cream one with the frill at the neck ...'

I searched her eyes – *The pink one with the zip at the back!* – for some sign that she was joking – *Stockings? High-heels?* – but there was nothing – *That cream one with the frill at the neck!* – except her wide-eyed, unflinching stare. Could she be as shocked and fascinated by the idea as I was? *A girl!* My sister was out of her mind.

'They wanted a girl anyway.' She took another kirby-grip from between her teeth and pressed it into place above my ear. Her voice sounded strange because of the kirby-grips, like a ventriloquist's.

'What d'you mean, wanted a girl?'

'Instead of a boy, that's all.'

I stared into the mirror. She had stopped being me a long time ago, this creature with the thick coating of coloured grease on her cheeks, the bright red lips and darkened eyebrows. She wasn't me, but she was. Every time I spoke, her lips moved.

'Who?' I said, watching the bright lips moving in the mirror.

Who? they seemed to be saying.

'Mum and dad,' said my sister, taking another kirby-grip from her mouth. She pressed it into place and added: 'I wish I had hair as thick as yours.'

'How d'you mean, wanted a girl instead of a boy?'

'Once they knew she was pregnant,' said my sister, standing back a moment to admire her handiwork in the mirror. 'I heard them saying they wanted it to be a girl. I wanted a sister too, you know. You came as a disappointment, I can tell you.'

'I couldn't choose what to be, could I?' I whined, staring in fascination at the bright lips. Had I said that, or had she? Was it my mouth, or hers?

'And you still can't,' said my sister. She picked up the hairbrush and began to brush the hair at the back of my head upwards. It felt all wrong.

'But that's different! Nobody can decide what to be before they get born!' I said, doubtfully. But what if people could? What if I had, and what if I'd decided wrong?

'I'm not saying anybody can. All I'm saying is you weren't what we were expecting. You weren't expected at all, if you want to know the truth. You were a mistake.'

'What d'you mean, a *mistake*?' The girl in the mirror raised her eyebrows, pouted her lips. And then the strangest thing happened – another mistake, maybe – and the girl in the mirror smiled at me. What did *she* have to smile about?

'I don't know what you're smiling at,' said my sister, 'it's true. Mum got pregnant by accident.'

By accident? I had heard different versions of how It could happen, but this was a new one on me: *by accident*.

'How do you mean?'

'I'm your big sister, am'n't I? I know things you don't, that's all. Mum and dad came up to me and they said, "How would you like to have a little sister?" Of course, I told them we couldn't afford it, but –'

'But why did they have one … I mean *me* … if you told them we … I mean *you* … couldn't afford …*it*?' My confusion as to what to call myself was made worse by the sight in the mirror. *It* seemed to be the best description.

'Because by that time it was *too late*. By that time she was pregnant, the damage was done.' She scattered the remaining kirby-grips on the glass-top of the dressing-table. The sound they made reminded me of the seeds scattering on the dinette linoleum and the hot, shivery feeling swept over me again ... I imagined being a tiny insect when its stone is lifted, running away from the giant's shadow ... Was I going to faint? (*Faint? Wasn't that what girls were supposed to do?*)

'What's the matter,' said my sister, 'don't you like it? Just the eyes to do now. Hold wide open.' She tilted my head back and began to attack my eyes with a little, evil-smelling, black brush. 'I wish I had lashes as long as yours,' she added.

'Wait till they *see!*' Wait till they *see.*' My sister clapped her hands in delight and hurried out of the room. I heard her squeaks of laughter as she ran downstairs. It sounded like a balloon being rubbed the wrong way. I wanted to run and hide, but it was difficult enough to stand still in my sister's high-heels. I hobbled around the room, then something drew me back to the mirror. I sat down and looked into it the way I'd seen my mother and my sister doing it, tilting my face this way and that, touching my hair here and there with a hand. The girl in the mirror smiled, but I felt more like screaming. (*Screaming? But wasn't that what girls ...?*) Now that I was alone with her, she seemed more monstrous than before. She swayed towards me and smiled her eerie smile again. And suddenly I knew what was so strange about her smile. It wasn't just that I didn't feel like smiling myself, though that was strange enough. No, the girl in the mirror was smiling *at herself*, pleased to see herself at last, smiling in triumph.

I stood up quickly and kicked off the shoes and ripped at the blouse, then the ill-feeling rose up inside me again as if I'd jumped off a roundabout. Then the world lurched and spun and all I knew was that I had to run, run because the stone had been lifted, run from the giant's shadow on the lino pretending to be wood in the dinette that wasn't the same thing as a dining room, run into the hallway where they stood at the top of the stairs, my mother with her hand flying up to her mouth letting out a whoop, my father forgetting to slouch because of what he saw with his eyes looking blue and amazed, run past them to the bathroom and the sink where I could let it all come up, hearing my father's rumbling laughter and my mother's whoops behind me and my sister's squeaking giggles like balloons, balloons with faces painted on them at the party, faces with faces painted on them at the party, faces of frogmen and astronauts and cowboys and pirates at the party, cakes and lemonade and sweets and games of musical chairs and blind-man's-buff and...I felt the cool hand on my burning forehead and I knew that I would never go now.

Story into Being
A Personal Essay

Sometimes I am asked where I get my ideas for stories. This is a question I have never been able to answer simply, because in my experience stories can be prompted by very diverse things. Indeed, sometimes I have no idea where the initial impetus (spur) to write a story comes from. A character, a place, an image or even just a phrase or two comes to me out of the blue, or from my subconscious, and I start from that, trying to work out if there really is a story here or not. Most often, there isn't. If there is, I have to discover what the story is and how it should be developed and resolved.

I'm not always sitting at a desk when I have this initial idea, of course. Sometimes, I'm sitting on a bus. All right, there I am on the bus thinking about nothing in particular, then an image takes shape in my mind: a woman with long straight hair, standing on a bridge, in the pouring rain. That's all that comes to me. I don't know who she is or what she's doing there. Assuming that I like the image or find it curious, I take another look at it. I notice that, despite the rain, the woman isn't wearing a coat or a jacket. She's going to catch her death if she goes on standing there, I think, and already I'm concerned about her, wondering what's going to happen to her or what she's going to do next. What happened to her coat?, I ask myself. Did she lose it? Did she run out of the house because she had had a row with her husband? Is she going to jump off that bridge?

Somehow I don't think she's the type to let herself contemplate suicide — she's too responsible. But she has reached a point in her life at which things have come to a head, that's obvious. She's reached the bridge and stopped there. Is she thinking about leaving her husband, then? But what about the kids?

And so I begin to draw on experience: not necessarily my personal experience — because I'm not a woman and I've never stood on a bridge in the rain without my coat — but my experience of people, of life, in order to make some sense of my initial image. I must also draw on experience of a different kind to make that bridge real, to describe it in such a way that a reader's imagination will recreate it just as I see it in my mind. Then I notice that I'm at my stop, so I get off the bus.

That is a crude account of how a story might begin. Stories don't always start with a mysterious image, however. Very often it's much more straightforward: something will happen to me or I'll witness something happening and I'll want to write about it. A story may also be sparked off by something I've read or heard about, or by something I remember. Even when the impetus of the story is clear, however, developing and resolving it is seldom a simple procedure. Even when a story is 'true' in the sense that it really happened, it's never a simple case of writing down what happened as accurately as possible, because in writing a story I'm trying to reach a different sort of truth — not the literal 'truth', but what might be called fictional truth. I think of the fictional truth as what really *should* happen in a story, as opposed to what really *did* happen in the incident or experience which may have prompted the story, and more than that: exactly *how* it should happen. To arrive at this kind of truth requires an effort of the imagination as well as the ability to be observant and accurate.

That is why I would shy away from describing any of my stories as autobiographical, even when a story is quite definitely based on the memory of a personal experience. The experience is always combined with other experiences and these autobiographical elements are changed imaginatively to suit the demands of the story, in the hope of arriving at that elusive, fictional truth.

'Anima' is a good example of this. I started from a memory.

I was eight or nine years old; I was upset because I had to go to a fancy dress party and I didn't know what to dress up as. My father made one or two impractical suggestions. In the end, my sisters dressed me up. The memory was vivid and I've learnt that vivid memories are sometimes worth exploring in writing, but it wasn't vivid in a detailed way. My memories usually aren't, but tend to be vaguely atmospheric. What was vivid was the feeling of being strangely upset about the whole business of dressing up for the party.

I started to describe the memory as best I could. I remembered sulking in the room we called 'the dinette' and very rarely used, then my father came in. Of course, I found that in order to describe it I had to start inventing things immediately, especially details. Parquet-style linoleum may very well have been the kind of linoleum in the room, but that's not the only reason it's there in the story. In fact, accuracy alone would not be a good enough reason to include such a detail. I brought this detail in because even at the outset the theme of the story was trying to emerge, though I didn't yet know what this was going to be. Similarly, it just seemed right that the boy in the story should notice a packet of seeds on the windowsill and pick it up. Only later, perhaps during the second draft, did I realise that in providing these concrete details my imagination was not only 'fleshing out' that room for the reader so that he would be able to see it in his mind, but was in fact selecting details which would, when gathered together, reinforce the whole point and theme of the story.

Even now, in retrospect, I would find it difficult to state the theme of 'Anima', but I know it has something to do with personal identity: how a person becomes the person he or she is, whether or not the person has any choice in the matter, and how people define each other.

During the initial stages of the writing, of course, I had no notion of a theme. But when I reached the point in the story at which the sister decides to use make-up on her little brother's eyes, I had an inkling of what the story was going to be about. It was at this point that the story 'took off' and departed radically from my memory. If I had been concerned about the literal truth, the boy in the story would have gone to the party dressed as a Chinaman, because that is what happened. But it seemed more apposite, and more daring, to dress *him* up as a girl and see how he would react, see what would happen. Having taken this risk, it became clearer to me why my imagination had offered me that parquet-linoleum, those seeds scattering like fleeing insects, the father's mock-anger and mock-laughter. Everything in the story was dressing up, trying to be something else, trying to find its identity.

Once I had this notion of what the story was about, I was in a position to revise it, adding details which had some bearing on this theme, anything which might reinforce it and enhance it, taking out anything which seemed irrelevant. In a short story, the more you can make everything — every event, every image, every word — *count* in this way, the stronger the story is likely to be.

BRIAN McCABE

*T*he Full Moon

'What is it?' asked the American lady. Unwittingly, she had voiced my thoughts — I was looking at her extravagant hairstyle and thinking exactly that: what *is* it? It looked like esparto grass trying to look like ice cream. But the enigma she was talking about was something of mine — a decoration I'd been making for the Halloween party in Ward One. I'd become so engrossed in the simple pleasure of making something that I'd scarcely noticed the visiting party. Besides, I had been working in the Therapy Unit for over a year and I'd come to regard the many visiting parties as something of an annoyance. I tended to ignore these processions of cheerful strangers — at times they made me think of sight-seeing tourists — and get on with what I was doing while the psychiatrists showed them round. The Halloween decoration had been coming along nicely: I'd cut out a large disc shape from a sheet of card. One side I'd painted black, the other I'd adorned with golden paper, cut to size. To the bright side I'd added, with glue and glitter, the image of a smiling face. Then I'd attached a long line of thread, so that it could be suspended from the ceiling in Ward One.

'It's the full moon,' I said.

She picked up the moon by its thread, then held it out at arm's length the better to appreciate it — and avoid the glue.

'My, it's gorgeous,' she said.

This was praise, but it was praise from a woman with a frightening hairstyle, wearing a lime-green twin-set. Pinned to her lapel there was a rectangular identity badge, and under the name I made out words which told me that she had come from the Psychology Department of an illegible university. She turned to one of her colleagues, a young man in a brown velvet suit, also sporting a badge.

'Ain't it cute?' she said to him. In the vicinity of his nose there grew a sparse mustache, which resembled the dirty marks often left by elastoplasts. His vague brown eyes tried to focus on my makeshift planet. Dangling from Twin-set's finger on its thread, it revolved of its own accord … now the dark side, now the bright.

'Yeah,' he said, 'what is it?' From the tone of his voice it was clear that he had been looking at people and their little achievements all day.

'It's the *moon!*' cooed Twin-set. She gave me a slow, sly wink which made me think of a television programme I had once seen, to do with the habits of lizards.

'Mmm,' said Mustache, 'quite a moon. You gonna put that gold stuff on this side too?' He was pointing to the side I'd painted black. My moon did a quick about-turn, as if to invalidate the question.

'That's the dark side,' I said. Twin-set gave out a short squeak of delight.

'Did you hear that?' she whispered excitedly. 'He says that's the *dark* side — ain't that adorable?'

I noticed that my status had changed, somewhere along the line, from the second to the third person singular. She gave me a benign smile, and as she laid my cardboard satellite on the table, she enunciated her praise volubly, as if she thought I might be deaf:

'It's a bee-oo-tiful moon!' she said.

I was beginning to wonder why so much was being made of what was, after all, only a decoration, when I felt the lady's hand gently patting the crown of my head. I felt a curious tingling all over my scalp, which then ran down the back of my neck and swarmed up and down my spine — a sensation I would normally associate with moments of acute embarrassment, anger, pleasure, or seeing ghosts. I was forced to realise it: *they thought I was one of the patients.*

It was the first time I had been taken for a bona-fide mental defective, and for an instant I caught a glimpse of what it was to be treated as such and I panicked. I stood up abruptly, causing the chair I'd been sitting on to crash to the floor behind me. Immediately, Johnny threw his paintbrush to the floor and ran out of the room, slamming the door as he went. Johnny was a patient with many eccentricities, personality disorders, ontological anxieties or call them what you will, and sometimes he would take a loud noise or a sudden movement to be an insult, directly aimed at his person. It had happened many times before, and I knew that he would run back to Ward One, then the nurses would calm him down and send him back to Therapy.

Mustache and Twin-set exchanged a meaningful glance, then I felt a hand on my shoulder.

'Sit down,' said Mustache, 'it's all right.' He righted my chair and pushed it into the backs of my legs. I looked around for another member of staff, but they had all gone into the Crafts Department with the other members of the visiting party.

'He's a bit jumpy,' said Twin-set, 'I think we should leave him alone.'

'We gotta be getting *along*,' said Mustache, unsure of how much of the message was getting through to me.

I raised my hand to detain them. I needed to explain. It was easy. All I had to say was: 'Actually, I'm not a patient at all; I'm a member of staff.' I might add, just for good measure, that I was in reality a Philosophy Graduate, working here in the Therapy Unit as a preventative expedient against unemployment. In my confusion I was able to utter three words. All three were monosyllabic, and I said them without much conviction:

'I ... work ... here,' I said.

'Sure you do,' said Mustache, 'siddown.'

'You should do some more work on that moon,' said Twin-set, 'I don't think it should have a dark side.'

She picked up the full moon and turned it over, so that it lay with the dark side up. Unaccountably, I did nothing to demonstrate my status as a sane, rational *employee*, but chose instead to reverse her action. I turned the moon over again, so that it lay with the bright side up. In its smiling golden face I saw my own features loom and distort.

'I figure he wants to keep one side of it black,' said Mustache.

I looked at his face, then Twin-set's, then his again. Both wore placatory smiles, but in their eyes I could read the vexation. It was as if I were a creature of a different species, one which might inhabit the dark side of the moon. I could not help myself — in a spasm of silent laughter, I sank weakly into the seat. I went on shuddering with laughter while, behind my back, they discussed me: what did I *have*? They spoke of Autism, Paranoia, Chronic Schizophrenia for all the world as if these were ailments people *had*, like measles! I wanted to correct them, I wanted to suggest that these were modes of being, that schizophrenia is something a person *is* ... but I was giggling like a maniac and, after all, irrational laughter could be the symptom of anything. But now my IQ was the moot point: was I low-grade, or high-grade?

'I don't know,' whispered Twin-set, 'but I'd sure like to look at his case-notes. Did you see the way he looked at us just then? He's weird.' My diagnosis had come: weird. A terminal case of weirdness.

'Mmm,' said Mustache, 'it makes you wonder what's going on inside his head. You know, I'm sure some of these people are in touch with things which are uh ... inaccessible to us, except maybe in dreams ...'

As my fit of laughter subsided, I noticed that Billy, sitting at the far end of the room, was sniggering into his hand. All the other patients — apart from Johnny, of course — had continued with their work in an orderly, methodical way, but Billy had been observing the whole episode and now he was sniggering conspicuously. The sight made me shudder slightly, because Billy had forgotten how to snigger — he was a patient who seldom spoke, or did anything at all of his own volition. He waited until he was told what to do, then he made his gesture of obedience. His apathy was almost impenetrable: he slouched in his seat, appeared to stare into space for hours, and often his mouth hung open. He looked always disconsolate, bored. I watched with growing fascination as he made some pretence of looking at his drawing, while his features contorted into this unaccustomed thing which looked like pain but wasn't. It was laughter. I had known him for over a year and it was the first time I had seen him laugh.

'That moon's amazing,' said Twin-set to Mustache. They were making for the door into the Crafts Department. 'You know that old wives' tale about how the full moon affects them?'

'Oh sure, I've heard about that.' Mustache gave a little laugh.

'Well, you wouldn't *believe* what one of the nurses in the wards was telling me today ...'

They waved their little bye-byes to me and closed the door behind them. My sanity was restored. On Billy's face there lingered an unmistakable smirk. Then less than a smirk, then nothing. I watched as his lower lip sagged, until his mouth hung open. He resumed his drawing, but his pencil scarcely touched the paper.

When I rang up Ward One, a nurse told me that Johnny had arrived in an agitated state.

'He said something about the full moon,' she said, 'but it isn't full just now, is it?'

'No, I'd been *making* a moon, out of card, and gold paper ... It's a decoration, you see, for the Halloween party in your ward.'

She made a small, non-commital noise.

'It's difficult to explain what happened,' I said. 'Is Johnny ready to come back over yet?'

'Oh, he's all right now. Mind you, some people say it does affect them.'

I mumbled something ungrammatical about people fearing madness more than death, then told her to send Johnny back to Therapy when he was ready.

I sat down at the table where I had been working. I turned the moon over and looked at the side I'd painted black. Perhaps it shouldn't have a dark side? I picked it up by its thread and held it out at arm's length. It turned, slowly ... now the bright side, now the dark. Billy looked up from his drawing, but his pencil went on whispering against the paper.

'Hey, Billy,' I said, 'ain't it cute?'

'Yeah,' he said quietly, 'what is it?'

BERNARD MACLAVERTY

S*ecrets*

He had been called to be there at the end. His Great Aunt Mary had been dying for some days now and the house was full of relatives. He had just left his girlfriend's home – they had been studying for 'A' levels together – and had come back to the house to find all the lights spilling onto the lawn and a sense of purpose which had been absent from the last few days.

He knelt at the bedroom door to join in the prayers. His knees were on the wooden threshold and he edged them forward onto the carpet. They had tried to wrap her fingers around a crucifix but they kept loosening. She lay low on the pillow and her face seemed to have shrunk by half since he had gone out earlier in the night. Her white hair was damped and pushed back from her forehead. She twisted her head from side to side, her eyes closed. The prayers chorused on, trying to cover the sound she was making deep in her throat. Someone said about her teeth and his mother leaned over her and said, 'That's the pet', and took her dentures from her mouth. The lower half of her face seemed to collapse. She half opened her eyes but could not raise her eyelids enough and showed only crescents of white.

'Hail Mary full of grace...' the prayers went on. He closed his hands over his face so that he would not have to look but smelt the trace of his girlfriend's handcream from his hands. The noise, deep and guttural, that his aunt was making became intolerable to him. It was as if she were drowning. She had lost all the dignity he knew her to have. He got up from the floor and stepped between the others who were kneeling and went into her sitting-room off the same landing.

He was trembling with anger or sorrow, he didn't know which. He sat in the brightness of her big sitting-room at the oval table and waited for something to happen. On the table was a cut-glass vase of irises, dying because she had been in bed for over a week. He sat staring at them. They were withering from the tips inward, scrolling themselves delicately, brown and neat. Clearing up after themselves. He stared at them for a long time until he heard the sounds of women weeping from the next room.

His aunt had been small – her head on a level with his when she sat at her table – and she seemed to get smaller each year. Her skin fresh, her hair white and waved and always well washed. She wore no jewelry except a cameo ring on the third finger of her right hand and, around her neck, a gold locket on a chain. The white classical profile on the ring was almost worn through and had become translucent and indistinct. The boy had noticed the ring when she had read to him as a child. In the beginning fairy tales, then as he got older extracts from famous novels, *Lorna Doone, Persuasion, Wuthering Heights* and her favourite extract, because she read it so often, Pip's meeting with Miss Havisham from *Great Expectations*. She would sit with him on her knee, her arms around him and holding the page flat with her hand. When he was bored he would interrupt her and ask about the ring. He loved hearing her tell of how her grandmother had given it to her as a brooch and she had had a ring made from it. He would try to count back to see how old it was. Had her grandmother got it from *her* grandmother? And if so what had she turned it into? She would nod her head from side to side and say, 'How would I know a thing like that?' keeping her place in the closed book with her finger.

'Don't be so inquisitive,' she'd say. 'Let's see what happens next in the story.'

One day she was sitting copying figures into a long narrow

book with a dip pen when he came into her room. She didn't look up but when he asked her a question she just said, 'Mm?' and went on writing. The vase of irises on the oval table vibrated slightly as she wrote.

'What is it?' She wiped the nib on blotting paper and looked up at him over her reading glasses.

'I've started collecting stamps and Mama says you might have some.'

'Does she now –?'

She got up from the table and went to the tall walnut bureau-bookcase standing in the alcove. From a shelf of the bookcase she took a small wallet of keys and selected one for the lock. There was a harsh metal shearing sound as she pulled the desk flap down. The writing area was covered with green leather which had dog-eared at the corners. The inner part was divided into pigeon holes, all bulging with papers. Some of them, envelopes, were gathered in batches nipped at the waist with elastic bands. There were postcards and bills and cash-books. She pointed to the postcards.

'You may have the stamps on those,' she said. 'But don't tear them. Steam them off.'

She went back to the oval table and continued writing. He sat on the arm of the chair looking through the picture postcards – torchlight processions at Lourdes, brown photographs of town centres, dull black and whites of beaches backed by faded hotels. Then he turned them over and began to sort the stamps. Spanish, with a bald man, French with a rooster, German with funny jerky print, some Italian with what looked like a chimney-sweep's bundle and a hatchet.

'These are great,' he said. 'I haven't got any of them.'

'Just be careful how you take them off.'

'Can I take them downstairs?'

'Is your mother there?'

'Yes.'

'Then perhaps it's best if you bring the kettle up here.'

He went down to the kitchen. His mother was in the morning room polishing silver. He took the kettle and the flex upstairs. Except for the dipping and scratching of his aunt's pen the room was silent. It was at the back of the house overlooking the orchard and the sound of traffic from the main road was distant and muted. A tiny rattle began as the kettle warmed up, then it bubbled and steam gushed quietly from its spout. The cards began to curl slightly in the jet of steam but she didn't seem to be watching. The stamps peeled moistly off and he put them in a saucer of water to flatten them.

'Who is Brother Benignus?' he asked. She seemed not to hear. He asked again and she looked over her glasses.

'He was a friend.'

His flourishing signature appeared again and again. Sometimes Bro Benignus, sometimes Benignus and once Iggy.

'Is he alive?'

'No, he's dead now. Watch the kettle doesn't run dry.'

When he had all the stamps off he put the postcards together and replaced them in the pigeon-hole. He reached over towards the letters but before his hand touched them his aunt's voice, harsh for once, warned.

'A-A-A,' she moved her pen from side to side. 'Do-not-touch.' she said and smiled. 'Anything else, yes! That section, no!' She resumed her writing.

The boy went through some other papers and found some photographs. One was a beautiful girl. It was very old-fashioned but he could see that she was beautiful. The picture was a pale brown oval set on a white square of card. The edges of the oval were misty. The girl in the photograph was young and had dark, dark hair scraped severely back and tied like a knotted rope on the top of her head – high arched eyebrows, her nose straight and thin, her mouth slightly smiling, yet not smiling – the way a mouth is after smiling. Her eyes looked out at him dark and knowing and beautiful.

'Who is that?' he asked.

'Why? What do you think of her?'

'She's all right.'

'Do you think she is beautiful?' The boy nodded.

'That's me,' she said. The boy was glad he had pleased her in return for the stamps.

Other photographs were there, not posed ones like Aunt Mary's but Brownie snaps of laughing groups of girls in bucket hats like German helmets and coats to their ankles. They seemed tiny faces covered in clothes. There was a photograph of a young man smoking a cigarette, his hair combed one way by the wind against a background of sea.

'Who is that in the uniform?' the boy asked.

'He's a soldier,' she answered without looking up.

'Oh,' said the boy. 'But who is he?'

'He was a friend of mine before you were born,' she said. Then added, 'Do I smell something cooking? Take your stamps and off you go. That's the boy.'

The boy looked at the back of the picture of the man and saw in black spidery ink 'John, Aug '15 Ballintoye'.

'I thought maybe it was Brother Benignus,' he said. She looked at him not answering.

'Was your friend killed in the war?'

At first she said no, but then she changed her mind.

'Perhaps he was,' she said, then smiled. 'You are far too inquisitive. Put it to use and go and see what is for tea. Your mother will need the kettle.' She came over to the bureau and helped tidy the photographs away. Then she locked it and put the keys on the shelf.

'Will you bring me up my tray?'

The boy nodded and left.

It was a Sunday evening, bright and summery. He was doing his homework and his mother was sitting on the carpet in one of her periodic fits of tidying out the drawers of the mahogany sideboard. On one side of her was a heap of paper scraps torn in quarters and bits of rubbish, on the other the useful items that had to be kept. The boy heard the bottom stair creak under Aunt Mary's light footstep. She knocked and put her head round the door and said that she was walking to Devotions. She was dressed in her good coat and hat and was just easing her fingers into her second glove. The boy saw her stop and pat her hair into place before the mirror in the hallway. His mother stretched over and slammed the door shut. It vibrated, then he heard the deeper sound of the outside door closing and her first few steps on the gravelled driveway. He sat for a long time wondering if he would have time or not. Devotions could take anything from twenty minutes to three quarters of an hour, depending on who was saying it.

Ten minutes must have passed, then the boy left his homework and went upstairs and into his aunt's sitting-room. He stood in front of the bureau wondering, then he reached for the keys. He tried several before he got the right one. The desk flap screeched as he pulled it down. He pretended to look at the postcards again in case there were any stamps he had missed. Then he put them away and reached for the bundle of letters. The elastic band was thick and old, brittle almost and when he took it off its track remained on the wad of letters. He carefully opened one and took out the letter and unfolded it, frail, khaki-coloured.

My dearest Mary, it began. I am so tired I can hardly write to you. I have spent what seems like all day censoring letters (there is a howitzer about 100 yds away firing every 2 minutes). The letters are heartrending in their attempt to express what they cannot. Some of the men are illiterate, others almost so. I know that they feel as much as we do, yet they do not have the words to express it. That is your job in the schoolroom to give us generations who can read and write well. They have...

The boy's eyes skipped down the page and over the next. He read the last paragraph.

Mary I love you as much as ever – more so that we cannot be together. I do not know which is worse, the hurt of this war or being separated from you. Give all my love to Brendan and all at home.

It was signed, scribbled with what he took to be John. He folded the paper carefully into its original creases and put it in the envelope. He opened another.

My love, it is thinking of you that keeps me sane. When I get a moment I open my memories of you as if I were reading. Your long dark hair – I always imagine you wearing the blouse with the tiny roses, the white one that opened down the back – your eyes that said so much without words, the way you lowered your head when I said anything that embarrassed you, and the clean nape of your neck.

The day I think about most was the day we climbed the head at Ballycastle. In a hollow, out of the wind, the air full of pollen and the sound of insects, the grass warm and dry and you lying beside me your hair undone, between me and the sun. You remember that that was where I first kissed you and the look of disbelief in your eyes that made me laugh afterwards.

It makes me laugh now to see myself savouring these memories standing alone up to my thighs in muck. It is everywhere, two, three feet deep. To walk ten yards leaves you quite breathless.

I haven't time to write more today so I leave you with my feet in the clay and my head in the clouds.

I love you, John.

He did not bother to put the letter back into the envelope but opened another.

My dearest, I am so cold that I find it difficult to keep my hand steady enough to write. You remember when we swam the last two fingers of your hand went the colour and texture of candles with the cold. Well that is how I am all over. It is almost four days since I had any real sensation in my feet or legs. Everything is frozen. The ground is like steel.

Forgive me telling you this but I feel I have to say it to someone. The worst thing is the dead. They sit or lie frozen in the position they died. You can distinguish them from the living because their faces are the colour of slate. God help us when the thaw comes ... This war is beginning to have an effect on me. I have lost all sense of feeling. The only emotion I have experienced lately is one of anger. Sheer white trembling anger. I have no pity or sorrow for the dead and injured. I thank God it is not me but I am enraged that it had to be them. If I live through this experience I will be a different person.

The only thing that remains constant is my love for you.

Today a man died beside me. A piece of shrapnel had

pierced his neck as we were moving under fire. I pulled him into a crater and stayed with him until he died. I watched him choke and then drown in his blood.

I am full of anger which has no direction.

He sorted through the pile and read half of some, all of others. The sun had fallen low in the sky and shone directly into the room onto the pages he was reading making the paper glare. He selected a letter from the back cf the pile and shaded it with his hand as he read.

Dearest Mary, I am writing this to you from my hospital bed. I hope that you were not too worried about not hearing from me. I have been here, so they tell me, for two weeks and it took another two weeks before I could bring myself to write this letter.

I have been thinking a lot as I lie here about the war and about myself and about you. I do not know how to say this but I feel deeply that I must do something, must sacrifice something to make up for the horror of the past year. In some strange way Christ has spoken to me through the carnage...

Suddenly the boy heard the creak of the stair and he frantically tried to slip the letter back into its envelope but it crumpled and would not fit. He bundled them all together. He could hear his aunt's familiar puffing on the short stairs to her room. He spread the elastic band wide with his fingers. It snapped and the letters scattered. He pushed them down into their pigeon hole and quickly closed the desk flap. The brass screeched loudly and clicked shut. At that moment his aunt came into the room.

'What are you doing boy?' she snapped.

'Nothing.' He stood with the keys in his hands. She walked to the bureau and opened it. The letters sprang out in an untidy heap.

'You have been reading my letters,' she said quietly. Her mouth was tight with the words and her eyes blazed. The boy could say nothing. She struck him across the side of the face.

'Get out,' she said. 'Get out of my room.'

The boy, the side of his face stinging and red, put the keys on the table on his way out. When he reached the door she called to him. He stopped, his hand on the handle.

'You are dirt,' she hissed, 'and always will be dirt. I shall remember this till the day I die.'

Even though it was a warm evening there was a fire in the large fireplace. His mother had asked him to light it so that she could clear out Aunt Mary's stuff. The room could then be his study, she said. She came in and seeing him at the table said, 'I hope I'm not disturbing you.'

'No.'

She took the keys from her pocket, opened the bureau and began burning papers and cards. She glanced quickly at each one before she flicked it onto the fire.

'Who was Brother Benignus?' he asked.

His mother stopped sorting and said, 'I don't know. Your aunt kept herself very much to herself. She got books from him through the post occasionally. That much I do know.'

She went on burning the cards. They built into strata, glowing red and black. Now and again she broke up the pile with the poker, sending showers of sparks up the chimney. He saw her come to the letters. She took off the elastic band and put it to one side with the useful things and began dealing the envelopes into the fire. She opened one and read quickly through it, then threw it on top of the burning pile.

'Mama,' he said.

'Yes?'

'Did Aunt Mary say anything about me?'

'What do you mean?'

'Before she died – did she say anything?'

'Not that I know of – the poor thing was too far gone to speak, God rest her.' She went on burning, lifting the corners of the letters with the poker to let the flames underneath them.

When he felt a hardness in his throat he put his head down on his books. Tears came into his eyes for the first time since she had died and he cried silently into the crook of his arm for the woman who had been his maiden aunt, his teller of tales, that she might forgive him.

GEORGE MACKAY BROWN

*S*ilver

'You'll never get her,' said the skipper of the *Kestrel*.

'She's meant for some rich farmer on the hill'. He shook his head.

The three other fishermen of the *Kestrel* shook their heads. 'You're too poor,' they said.

Bert the cook laughed sarcastically.

I took the three best haddocks I could find from the morning's catch and set out for the farm.

They shook their heads after me. The skipper took his pipe from his mouth and spat – he thought I must have gone out of my mind.

I was astonished at my own resolution. Was I not the shy one of the *Kestrel*, who dodged into the wheelhouse whenever a pretty girl stood on the pier above and asked were there any scallops to spare?

I walked on through the village with my three sklintering haddocks.

For the first time – between the tailor shop and the kirk – I felt a flutter of fear. The farm I was going to – it was said that queer proud cantankerous folk lived on it. What could a shy fisherman say to the likes of them, with their hills of green and yellow and their ancestors going back to the days of King Hakon?

That stern tree had lately burgeoned with Anna.

For the love of Anna I was approaching Muckle Glebe.

Old Check was taking the shutters from the hotel bar as I went past. It was opening time in the village.

I stood in need of a glass of rum to feed my faltering flame.

'Well', said the old landlord, as he set the rum before me and took my silver, 'they're still at it. Belfast. Viet-Nam. The Jews and the Arabs. And now Iceland.'

Poor old Check, I thought to myself, worrying about troubles he can do nothing to put right. How terrible to be old, and your heart as dry as a cork!

'Well,' I said, drinking down the last of the rum, 'but there must be love songs even in places like that.'

He looked at me as if I was mad. One or two villagers came into the bar. I went out.

As I left the last houses of the village the small simple-witted boy called Oik who lives with his mother and three or four illegitimate brothers and sisters in a war-time hut ran after me. The story is that a horse kicked him. If so, that beast set a spark of great innocence adrift on the world.

'O mister,' he said, 'where are you going?'

I said I was going to Anna of Muckle Glebe. No point in dissimulating with a boy like Oik.

'Are you going to give Anna them fish?' he said. He looked at the haddocks with round pellucid hungry eyes.

I said it was a present for Anna.

'Anna's the nicest lass in Norday,' said Oik. 'But she tells terrible lies.'

This mingled estimate of Anna's character, coming from such an innocent mouth, intrigued me. I stopped in my tracks and looked at the boy.

'Besides,' said Oik, 'they don't need fish up at Muckle Glebe.'

The three haddocks flashed in the sun. 'Maybe two would be enough for a place like that,' I said. I loosened the string and freed a jaw and gave the smallest fish to Oik.

'Now tell me,' I said, 'what kind of lies does Anna tell?'

But he was off. He did not even pause to thank me. His bare legs flickered across the field. The dog leapt out of the hut to meet him, barking. 'O mam,' he shouted, 'look what I got!

That man from the *Kestrel* has give me a fish!'

I went on till I was out of hearing of the sounds of wonderment and barking.

Quite apart from Anna, I was going to Muckle Glebe to get my silver chain back. Anna had taken it from my neck, between kisses, at the dance on Friday night in the community centre. It was the chain my mother gave me on my seventeenth birthday in January. 'Come up to the farm Thursday morning,' Anna whispered. 'They're all going to the mart in Kirkwall. We'll be alone. You'll get your chain back then. And something to go with it far more precious, precious. You can bring a fish too, if you like' ... And she had sealed the bargain with another marvellous kiss.

I knew then that I could marry no other girl in the world but Anna. The very thought of her, all that week, had been enough to set my spirit trembling.

But how could poverty like mine ever fall like a blessing on that proud house?

My feet went on more slowly.

The shop of Mrs Thomasina Skerry – coats, corned beef, spades, cups, coffee, whisky, salt fish, tobacco, sweets, stamps, newspapers, all in one withered drab hut – stood at the crossroads.

I went in for a packet of fags.

'I like a fish,' said Thomasina, eyeing the couple of slaughtered beauties that swung from my forefinger. I laid them on the floor, out of the way of her all-devouring eye.

'It isn't often we see a Selskay man in this part of the island,' she said. 'I like nothing better than a bit of boiled haddock and butter to my tea.'

I was talking – I knew it – to the most talented gossip in Norday. Certain information about a certain farm could be traded for a firm fresh haddock, I hoped. (The *Kestrel*, I should explain, visits this island only rarely – we come from Selskay, further to the west – about Norday we know only rumours and legends.) But, even from the warped mouth behind the counter the very names "Muckle Glebe" and "Anna" would come like music: whatever she might say about them.

'I have a message,' I said, 'to a big farm a mile further on.'

'Muckle Glebe,' she said. 'Muckle Glebe. The Taings – a proud lot. A cut above the ordinary. O, very hoity toity – you would think they were gentry, or something. Let me tell you, they have their faults and their failings like everybody else. The great-grandfather of the present Taing was an orra-boy, a dung spreader. O, I could tell you a thing or two...I haven't been keeping well in my health lately – my stomach – "a light diet", Dr Scott says – "fish, for example", he says.'

'Maybe what you say is true,' I said, 'or maybe it isn't, but there's one member of that family that no tongue could ever blacken, and that's Anna Taing'... My lips trembled as I pronounced the blessed name.

Mistress Skerry's eyes widened. 'O, is that so!' she cried. 'Indeed! Anna Taing. I could tell you things about Anna Taing, mister. But I'm saying nothing. It's best to keep silence. In this island the truth isn't welcome. My tongue, it's got me into trouble before now...The great thing with fish is that you can use the water you boil it in for soup, and make patties with the leftover bits. The cat, he generally eats the head.'

'What you say,' I said, 'will go no further'...And I bent down and freed another haddock-jaw from the string and held it up among her sweetie-jars and loaves and fair-isle jerseys.

We admired the beautiful silver-grey shape together for three long seconds.

'Well,' she said. 'I'll tell you. It's general knowledge anyway.'

The fish was hers. She laid it on an old newspaper behind the counter – wiped her hands on her apron – licked her lips – and told me a bad story.

A student from Edinburgh had worked all last summer at Muckle Glebe, from hay-time to harvest. Whenever he got leave to work, that is, for wasn't that little tart of an Anna running after him from field to byre, and more than running after him once it got dark and the farm work was done. Thomasina had heard it from this customer and that, but she saw the proof of it herself at the Agricultural Show. Hundreds of folk there, going and coming; and there, in the midst of all the people and animals, in the broad light of noon, stood Anna of Muckle Glebe and the student, with their arms tight around one another, and kissing every minute regularly as if to make sure their mouths were still there. Love is for night and the stars. It had been a public disgrace.

But then, Anna Taing was and always had been a man-mad little slut. There was hardly a lad in the island that hadn't been out with her. She would go with any Tom, Dick or Harry. There was that hawker that had been in the island – a right low-looking tyke – wasn't she seen knocking at his caravan door at midnight one night...

But she still wrote to this student. She still kept up with him. And the folk up at Muckle Glebe, they were right pleased whenever the typed letters with the Edinburgh post-mark came. 'Because, you see,' said Mrs Thomasina Skerry, 'they're a nest of snobs up at that place, and what a grand catch it would be for their Anna – somebody who's going to be a lawyer or a doctor.'

Her rapturous narrative over, she counselled me, whatever my business was at Muckle Glebe, not to breathe a syllable of what she had said.

My throat worked on this gall for a full minute.

'You're nothing but a damned old scandal-monger,' I shouted. And picked up the sole remaining haddock. And made haste to shake the dust of bananas and wheat and cloves and tea and wool from my feet. And left a patch of slime on her shop floor.

At the door of the farm of Muckle Glebe I set down my gift and knocked. No one answered, but I had the feeling that eyes were watching from curtain edges. I knocked again. (Surely there was no duplicity in the true gentle fun-loving heart that had unfolded itself to me at the dance in the community centre – it was impossible – and the world was full of evil old hags.) I knocked again.

This time the door was opened by a young woman – a sister, obviously, and about six sour years older.

She gave me the coldest of looks.

I asked for Anna.

I felt immediately what impudence it was for a common fisherman to come enquiring about one of the daughters of this ancient farm that had a coat-of-arms carved over the lintel.

'My sister Anna,' she said, 'flew to Kirkwall this morning. From Kirkwall she will be flying to Edinburgh. In Edinburgh, for your information, she is to be engaged to Mr Andrew Blair, a veterinary student. It will be announced in "The Scotsman".'

I mentioned, trembling, a silver chain. She said she knew nothing about silver chains.

She shut the door in my face. When I turned to go, I discovered that the four cats of Muckle Glebe had reduced the firmest and fattest of my haddocks to a jagged skeleton.

GEORGE MACKAY BROWN

The Wireless Set

The first wireless ever to come to the valley of Tronvik in Orkney was brought by Howie Eunson, son of Hugh the fisherman and Betsy.

Howie had been at the whaling in the Antarctic all winter, and he arrived back in Britain in April with a stuffed wallet and jingling pockets. Passing through Glasgow on his way home he bought presents for everyone in Tronvik – fiddle-strings for Sam down at the shore, a bottle of malt whisky for Mansie of the hill, a second-hand volume of Spurgeon's sermons for Mr Sinclair the missionary, sweeties for all the bairns, a meerschaum pipe for his father Hugh and a portable wireless set for his mother Betsy.

There was great excitement the night Howie arrived home in Tronvik. Everyone in the valley – men, women, children, dogs, cats – crowded into the butt-end of the croft, as Howie unwrapped and distributed his gifts.

'And have you been a good boy all the time you've been away?' said Betsy anxiously. 'Have you prayed every night, and not sworn?'

'This is thine, mother,' said Howie, and out of a big cardboard box he lifted the portable wireless and set it on the table.

For a full two minutes nobody said a word. They all stood staring at it, making small round noises of wonderment, like pigeons.

'And mercy,' said Betsy at last, 'what is it at all?'

'It's a wireless set,' said Howie proudly. 'Listen.'

He turned a little black knob and a posh voice came out of the box saying that it would be a fine day tomorrow over England, and over Scotland south of the Forth-Clyde valley, but that in the Highlands and in Orkney and Shetland there would be rain and moderate westerly winds.

'If it's a man that's speaking', said old Hugh doubtfully, 'where is he standing just now?'

'In London,' said Howie.

'Well now,' said Betsy, 'if that isn't a marvel! But I'm not sure, all the same, but what it isn't against the scriptures. Maybe, Howie, we'd better not keep it.'

'Everybody in the big cities has a wireless,' said Howie. 'Even in Kirkwall and Hamnavoe every house has one. But now Tronvik has a wireless as well, and maybe we're not such clodhoppers as they think.'

They all stayed late, listening to the wireless. Howie kept twirling a second little knob, and sometimes they would hear music, and sometimes they would hear a kind of loud half-witted voice urging them to use a particular brand of tooth-paste.

At half past eleven the wireless was switched off and everybody went home. Hugh and Betsy and Howie were left alone.

'Men speak,' said Betsy, 'but it's hard to know sometimes whether what they say is truth or lies.'

'This wireless speaks the truth,' said Howie.

Old Hugh shook his head. 'Indeed,' he said, 'it doesn't do that. For the man said there would be rain here and a westerly wind. But I assure you it'll be a fine day, and a southerly wind, and if the Lord spares me I'll get to the lobsters.'

Old Hugh was right. Next day was fine, and he and Howie took twenty lobsters from the creels he had under the Gray Head.

It was in the spring of the year 1939 that the first wireless set came to Tronvik. In September that same year war broke out, and Howie and three other lads from the valley joined the minesweepers.

That winter the wireless standing on Betsy's table became the centre of Tronvik. Every evening folk came from the crofts to listen to the nine o'clock news. Hitherto the wireless had been a plaything which discoursed Scottish reels and constipation advertisements and unreliable weather forecasts. But now the whole world was embattled and Tronvik listened appreciatively to enthusiastic commentators telling them that General Gamelin was the greatest soldier of the century, and he had only to say the word for the German Siegfried Line to crumble like sand. In the summer of 1940 the western front flared into life, and then suddenly no more was heard of General Gamelin. First it was General Weygand who was called the heir of Napoleon, and then a few days later Marshal Petain.

France fell all the same, and old Hugh turned to the others and said, 'What did I tell you? You can't believe a word it says'.

One morning they saw a huge gray shape looming along the horizon, making for Scapa Flow. 'Do you ken the name of that warship?' said Mansie of the hill. 'She's the *Ark Royal*, an aircraft carrier.'

That same evening Betsy twiddled the knob of the wireless and suddenly an impudent voice came drawling out. The voice was saying that German dive bombers had sunk the *Ark Royal* in the Mediterranean. 'Where is the *Ark Royal*?' went the voice in an evil refrain. 'Where is the *Ark Royal*?' Where is the *Ark Royal*?'

'That man,' said Betsy 'must be the Father of Lies.'

Wasn't the *Ark Royal* safely anchored in calm water on the other side of the hill?

Thereafter the voice of Lord Haw-Haw cast a spell on the inhabitants of Tronvik. The people would rather listen to him than to anyone, he was such a great liar. He had a kind of bestial joviality about him that at once repelled and fascinated them; just as, for opposite reasons, they had been repelled and fascinated to begin with by the rapturous ferocity of Mr Sinclair's Sunday afternoon sermons, but had grown quite pleased with them in time.

They never grew pleased with William Joyce, Lord Haw-Haw. Yet every evening found them clustered round the portable radio, like awed children round a hectoring schoolmaster.

'Do you know,' said Sam of the shore one night, 'I think that man will come to a bad end.'

Betsy was frying bloody-puddings over a primus stove, and the evil voice went on and on against a background of hissing, sputtering, roaring and a medley of rich succulent smells.

Everyone in the valley was there that night. Betsy had made some new ale and the first bottles were being opened. It was good stuff, right enough; everybody agreed about that.

Now the disembodied voice paused, and turned casually to a new theme, the growing starvation of the people of Britain. The food ships were being sunk one after the other by the heroic U-boats. Nothing was getting through, nothing, nor a cornstalk from Saskatchewan nor a tin of pork from Chicago. Britain was starving. The war would soon be over. Then there would be certain pressing accounts to meet. The ships were going down. Last week the Merchant Navy was poorer by a half million gross registered tons. Britain was starving –

At this point Betsy, who enjoyed her own ale more than anyone else, thrust the hissing frying pan under the nose – so to speak – of the wireless, so that its gleam was dimmed for a moment or two by a rich blue tangle of bloody-pudding fumes.

'Smell that, you brute,' cried Betsy fiercely, 'smell that!'

The voice went on, calm and vindictive.

'Do you ken,' said Hugh, 'he canna hear a word you're saying.'

'Can he not?' said Sandy Omand, turning his taurine head from one to the other. 'He canna hear?'

Sandy was a bit simple.

'No,' said Hugh, 'nor smell either.'

After that they switched off the wireless, and ate the bloody-puddings along with buttered bannocks, and drank more ale, and told more stories that had nothing to do with war, till two o'clock in the morning.

One afternoon in the late summer of that year the island postman cycled over the hill road to Tronvik with a yellow corner of telegram sticking out of his pocket.

He passed the shop and the manse and the schoolhouse, and went in a wavering line up the track to Hugh's croft. The wireless was playing music inside, Joe Loss and his orchestra.

Betsy had seen him coming and was standing in the door.

'Is there anybody with you?' said the postman.

'What way would there be?' said Betsy. 'Hugh's at the lobsters.'

'There should be somebody with you,' said the postman.

'Give me the telegram,' said Betsy, and held out her hand. He gave it to her as if he was a miser parting with a twenty-pound note.

She went inside, put on her spectacles, and ripped open the envelope with brisk fingers. Her lips moved a little silently reading the words.

Then she turned to the dog and said, 'Howie's dead.' She went to the door. The postman was disappearing on his bike round the corner of the shop and the missionary was hurrying towards her up the path.

She said to him, 'It's time the peats were carted.'

'This is a great affliction, you poor soul,' said Mr Sinclair the missionary. 'This is bad news indeed. Yet he died for his country. He made the great sacrifice. So that we could all live in peace, you understand.'

Betsy shook her head. 'That isn't it at all,' she said. 'Howie's sunk with torpedoes. That's all I know.'

They saw old Hugh walking up from the shore with a pile of creels on his back and a lobster in each hand. When he came to the croft he looked at Betsy and the missionary standing together in the door. He went into the outhouse and set down the creels and picked up an axe he kept for chopping wood.

Betsy said to him, 'How many lobsters did you get?'

He moved past her and the missionary without speaking into the house. Then from inside he said, 'I got two lobsters.'

'I'll break the news to him,' said Mr Sinclair.

From inside came the noise of shattering wood and metal.

'He knows already,' said Betsy to the missionary. 'Hugh knows the truth of a thing generally before a word is uttered.'

Hugh moved past them with the axe in his hand.

'I got six crabs forby,' he said to Betsy, 'but I left them in the boat.'

He set the axe down carefully inside the door of the outhouse. Then he leaned against the wall and looked out to sea for a long while.

'I got thirteen eggs,' said Betsy. 'One more than yesterday. That old Rhode Islander's laying like mad.'

The missionary was slowly shaking his head in the doorway. He touched Hugh on the shoulder and said, 'My poor man–'

Hugh turned and said to him, 'It's time the last peats were down from the hill. I'll go in the morning first thing. You'll be needing a cart-load for the Manse.'

The missionary, awed by such callousness, walked down the path between the cabbages and potatoes. Betsy went into the house. The wireless stood, a tangled wreck, on the dresser. She brought from the cupboard a bottle of whisky and glasses. She set the kettle on the hook over the fire and broke the peats into red and yellow flame with a poker. Through the window she could see people moving towards the croft from all over the valley. The news had got round. The mourners were gathering.

Old Hugh stood in the door and looked up at the drift of clouds above the cliff. 'Yes,' he said, 'I'm glad I set the creels where I did, off Yesnaby. They'll be sheltered there once the wind gets up.'

'That white hen,' said Betsy, 'has stopped laying. It's time she was in the pot, if you ask me.'

GEORGE MACKAY BROWN

*A*ndrina

Andrina comes to see me every afternoon in winter, just before it gets dark. She lights my lamp, sets the peat fire in a blaze, sees that there is enough water in my bucket that stands on the wall niche. If I have a cold (which isn't often, I'm a tough old seaman) she fusses a little, puts an extra peat or two on the fire, fills a stone hot-water bottle, puts an old thick jersey about my shoulders.

That good Andrina – as soon as she has gone, after her occasional ministrations to keep pleurisy or pneumonia away – I throw the jersey from my shoulders and mix myself a toddy, whisky and hot water and sugar. The hot water bottle in the bed will be cold long before I climb into it, round about midnight: having read my few chapters of Conrad.

Towards the end of February last year I did get a very bad cold, the worst for years. I woke up, shuddering, one morning, and crawled between fire and cupboard, gasping like a fish out of water, to get a breakfast ready. (Not that I had an appetite.) There was a stone lodged somewhere in my right lung, that blocked my breath.

I forced down a few tasteless mouthfulls, and drank hot ugly tea. There was nothing to do after that but get back to bed with my book. Reading was no pleasure either – my head was a block of pulsing wood.

'Well,' I thought, 'Andrina'll be here in five or six hours' time. She won't be able to do much for me. This cold, or flu, or whatever it is, will run its course. Still, it'll cheer me to see the girl.'

Andrina did not come that afternoon. I expected her with the first cluster of shadows: the slow lift of the latch, the low greeting, the 'tut-tut' of sweet disapproval at some of the things she saw as soon as the lamp was burning...I was, though, in that strange fatalistic mood that sometimes accompanies a fever, when a man doesn't really care what happens. If the house was to go on fire, he might think, 'What's this, flames?' and try to save himself: but it wouldn't horrify or thrill him.

I accepted that afternoon, when the window was blackness at last with a first salting of stars, that for some reason or another Andrina couldn't come. I fell asleep again.

I woke up. A gray light at the window. My throat was dry – there was a fire in my face – my head was more throbbingly wooden than ever. I got up, my feet flashing with cold pain on the stone floor, drank a cup of water, and climbed back into bed. My teeth actually clacked and chattered in my head for five minutes or more – a thing I had only read about before.

I slept again, and woke up just as the winter sun was making brief stained glass of sea and sky. It was, again, Andrina's time. Today there were things she could do for for me: get aspirin from the shop, surround my grayness with three or four very hot bottles, mix the strongest toddy in the world. A few words from her would be like a bell-buoy to a sailor lost in a hopeless fog. She did not come.

She did not come again on the third afternoon.

I woke, tremblingly, like a ghost in a hollow stone. It was black night. Wind soughed in the chimney. There was, from time to time, spatters of rain against the window. It was the longest night of my life. I experienced, over again, some of the dull and sordid events of my life; one certain episode was repeated again and again like an ancient gramophone record being put on time after time, and a rusty needle scuttling over worn wax. The shameful images broke and melted at last into sleep. Love had been killed but many ghosts had been awakened.

When I woke up I heard, for the first time in four days, the sound of a voice. It was Stanley the postman speaking to the dog of Bighouse. 'There now, isn't that loud big words to say so early? It's just a letter for Minnie, a drapery catalogue. There's a good boy, go and tell Minnie I have a love letter for her...Is that you, Minnie? I thought old Ben here was going to tear me in pieces then. Yes, Minnie, a fine morning, it is that...'

I have never liked that postman – a servile lickspittle to anyone he thinks is of consequence in the island – but that morning he came past my window like a messenger of light. He opened the door without knocking (I am a person of small consequence). He said, 'Letter from a long distance, skipper.' He put the letter on the chair nearest the door. I was shaping my mouth to say, 'I'm not very well. I wonder...' If words did come out of my mouth, they must have been whispers, a ghost appeal. He looked at the dead fire and the closed window. He said, 'Phew! It's fuggy in here, skipper. You want to get some fresh air...' Then he went, closing the door behind him (He would not, as I had briefly hoped, be taking word to Andrina, or the doctor down in the village.)

I imagined, until I drowsed again, Captain Scott writing his few last words in the Antarctic tent.

In a day or two, of course, I was as right as rain; a tough old salt like me isn't killed off that easily.

But there was a sense of desolation on me. It was as if I had been betrayed – deliberately kicked when I was down. I came almost to the verge of self-pity. Why had my friend left me in my bad time?

Then good sense asserted itself. 'Torvald, you old fraud,' I said to myself. 'What claim have you got, anyway, on a winsome twenty-year old? None at all. Look at it this way, man – you've had a whole winter of her kindness and consideration. She brought a lamp into your dark time: ever since the Harvest Home when (like a fool) you had too much whisky and she supported you home and rolled you unconscious into bed... Well, for some reason or another Andrina hasn't been able to come these last few days. I'll find out, today, the reason.'

It was high time for me to get to the village. There was not a crust or scraping of butter or jam in the cupboard. The shop was also the Post Office – I had to draw two weeks' pension. I promised myself a pint or two in the pub, to wash the last of that sickness out of me.

It struck me, as I trudged those two miles, that I knew nothing about Andrina at all. I had never asked, and she had said nothing. What was her father? Had she sisters and brothers? Even the district of the island where she lived had never cropped up in our talks. It was sufficient that she came every evening, soon after sunset, and performed her quiet ministrations, and lingered awhile; and left a peace behind – a sense that everything in the house was pure, as if it had stood with open doors and windows at the heart of a clean summer wind.

Yet the girl had never done, all last winter, asking me questions about myself – all the good and bad and exciting things that had happened to me. Of course I told her this and that. Old men love to make their past vivid and significant, to stand in relation to a few trivial events in as fair and bold a light as possible. To add spice to those bits of autobiography, I let on to have been a reckless wild daring lad – a known and somewhat feared figure in many a port from Hong Kong to Durban to San Francisco. I presented to her a character somewhere between Captain Cook and Captain Hook.

And the girl loved these pieces of mingled fiction and fact; turning the wick of my lamp down a little to make everything more mysterious, stirring the peats into new flowers of flame...

One story I did not tell her completely. It is the episode in my life that hurts me whenever I think of it (which is rarely, for that time is locked up and the key dropped deep in the Atlantic: but it haunted me – as I hinted – during my recent illness).

On her last evening at my fireside I did, I know, let drop a hint or two to Andrina – a few half-ashamed half-boastful fragments. Suddenly, before I had finished – as if she could foresee and suffer the end – she had put a white look and cold kiss on my cheek, and gone out at the door; as it turned out, for the last time.

Hurt or no, I will mention it here and now. You who look and listen are not Andrina – to you it will seem a tale of crude country manners: a mingling of innocence and heartlessness.

In the island, fifty years ago, a young man and a young woman came together. They had known each other all their lives up to then, of course – they had sat in the school room together – but on one particular day in early summer this boy from one croft and this girl from another distant croft looked at each other with new eyes.

After the midsummer dance in the barn of the big house, they walked together across the hill through the lingering enchantment of twilight – it is never dark then – and came to the rocks and the sand and sea just as the sun was rising. For an hour and more they lingered, tranced creatures indeed, beside those bright sighings and swirlings. Far in the north-east the springs of day were beginning to surge up.

It was a tale soaked in the light of a single brief summer. The boy and the girl lived, it seemed, on each other's heartbeats. Their parents' crofts were miles apart, but they contrived to meet, as if by accident, most days; at the crossroads, in the village shop, on the side of the hill. But really these places were too earthy and open – there were too many windows – their feet drew secretly night after night to the beach with its bird-cries, its cave, its changing waters. There no one disturbed their communings – the shy touches of hand and mouth – the words that were nonsense but that became in his mouth sometimes a sweet mysterious music – 'Sigrid'.

The boy – his future, once this idyll of a summer was ended, was to go to the university in Aberdeen and there study to be a man of security and position and some leisure – an estate his crofting ancestors had never known.

No such door was to open for Sigrid – she was bound to the few family acres – the digging of peat – the making of butter and cheese. But for a short time only. Her place would be beside the young man with whom she shared her breath and heartbeats, once he had gained his teacher's certificate. They walked day after day beside shining beckoning waters.

But one evening, at the cave, towards the end of that summer, when the corn was taking a first burnish, she had something urgent to tell him – a tremulous perilous secret thing. And at once the summertime spell was broken. He shook his head. He looked away. He looked at her again as if she were some slut who had insulted him. She put out her hand to him, her mouth trembling. He thrust her away. He turned. He ran up the beach and along the sand-track to the road above; and the ripening fields gathered him soon and hid him from her.

And the girl was left alone at the mouth of the cave, with the burden of a greater more desolate mystery on her.

The young man did not go to any seat of higher learning. That same day he was at the emigration agents in Hamnavoe, asking for an urgent immediate passage to Canada or Australia or South Africa – anywhere.

Thereafter the tale became complicated and more cruel and pathetic still. The girl followed him as best she could to his transatlantic refuge a month or so later; only to discover that the bird had flown. He had signed on a ship bound for furthest ports, as an ordinary seaman: so she was told, and she was more utterly lost than ever.

That rootlessness, for the next half century, was to be his life: making salt circles about the globe, with no secure footage anywhere. To be sure, he studied his navigation manuals, he rose at last to be a ship's officer, and more. The barren years became a burden to him. There is a time, when white hairs come, to turn one's back on long and practised skills and arts, that have long since lost their savours. This the sailor did, and he set his course homeward to his island; hoping that fifty winters might have scabbed over an old wound.

And so it was, or seemed to be. A few remembered him vaguely. The name of a certain vanished woman – who must be elderly, like himself, now – he never mentioned, nor did he ever hear it uttered. Her parents' croft was a ruin, a ruckle of stones on the side of the hill. He climbed up to it one day and looked at it coldly. No sweet ghost lingered at the end of the house, waiting for a twilight summons – 'Sigrid...'

I got my pension cashed, and a basket full of provisions, in the village shop. Tina Stewart the postmistress knew everybody and everything; all the shifting subtle web of relationships in the island. I tried devious approaches with her. What was new or strange in the island? Had anyone been taken suddenly ill? Had anybody – a young woman, for example – had to leave the island suddenly, for whatever reason? The hawk eye of Miss Stewart regarded me long and hard. No, said she, she had never known the island quieter. Nobody had come or gone. 'Only yourself, Captain Torvald, has been bedridden, I hear. You better take good care of yourself, you all alone up there. There's still grayness in your face...' I said I was sorry to take her time up. Somebody had mentioned a name – Andrina – to me, in a certain connection. It was a matter of no importance. Could Miss Stewart, however, tell me which farm or croft this Andrina came from?

Tina looked at me a long while, then shook her head. There was nobody of that name – woman or girl or child – in the island; and there never had been, to her certain knowledge.

I paid for my messages, with trembling fingers, and left.

I felt the need of a drink. At the bar counter stood Isaac Irving the landlord. Two fishermen stood at the far end, next to the fire, drinking their pints and playing dominoes.

I said, after the third whisky, 'Look, Isaac, I suppose the whole island knows that Andrina – that girl – has been coming all winter up to my place, to do a bit of cleaning and washing and cooking for me. She hasn't been for a week now and more. Do you know if there's anything the matter with her? (What I dreaded to hear was that Andrina had suddenly fallen in love; her little rockpools of charity and kindness drowned in that huge incoming flood; and had cloistered herself against the time of her wedding.)

Isaac looked at me as if I was out of my mind. 'A young woman,' said he. 'A young woman up at your house? A home help, is she? I didn't know you had a home help. How many whiskies did you have before you came here, skipper, eh?' And he winked at the two grinning fishermen over by the fire.

I drank down my fourth whisky and prepared to go.

'Sorry, skipper,' Isaac Irving called after me. 'I think you must have imagined that girl, whatever her name is, when the fever was on you. Sometimes that happens. The only women

I saw when I had the flu were hags and witches. You're lucky, skipper – a honey like Andrina!'

I was utterly bewildered. Isaac Irving knows the island and its people, if anything, even better than Tina Stewart. And he is a kindly man, not given to making fools of the lost and the delusion-ridden.

Going home, March airs were moving over the island. The sky, almost overnight, was taller and bluer. Daffodils trumpeted, silently, the entry of spring from ditches here and there. A young lamb danced, all four feet in the air at once.

I found, lying on the table, unopened, the letter that had been delivered three mornings ago. There was an Australian postmark. It had been posted in late October.

'I followed your young flight from Selskay half round the world, and at last stopped here in Tasmania, knowing that it was useless for me to go any further. I have kept a silence too, because I had such regard for you that I did not want you to suffer as I had, in many ways, over the years. We are both old, maybe I am writing this in vain, for you might never have returned to Selskay; or you might be dust or salt. I think, if you are still alive and (it may be) lonely, that what I will write might gladden you, though the end of it is sadness, like so much of life. Of your child – our child – I do not say anything, because you did not wish to acknowledge her. But that child had, in her turn, a daughter, and I think I have seen such sweetness but rarely. I thank you that you, in a sense (though unwillingly), gave that light and goodness to my age. She would have been a lamp in your winter, too, for often I spoke to her about you and that long-gone summer we shared, which was, to me at least, such a wonder. I told her nothing of the end of that time, that you and some others thought to be shameful. I told her only things that came sweetly from my mouth. And she would say, often, 'I wish I knew that grandfather of mine. Gran, do you think he's lonely? I think he would be glad of somebody to make him a pot of tea and see to his fire. Some day I'm going to Scotland and I'm going to knock on his door, wherever he lives, and I'll do things for him. Did you love him very much, gran? He must be a good person, that old sailor, ever to have been loved by you. I *will* see him. I'll hear the old stories from his own mouth. Most of all, of course, the love story – for you, gran tell me nothing about that...' I am writing this letter, Bill, to tell you that this can never now be. Our granddaughter Andrina died last week, suddenly, in the first stirrings of spring...'

Later, over the fire, I thought of the brightness and burgeoning and dew that visitant had brought across the threshold of my latest winter, night after night; and of how she had always come with the first shadows and the first star; but there, where she was dust, a new time was brightening earth and sea.

T he Art of Narrative

A Personal Essay

Writers like me who live in a group of islands might seem to be cut off from contact with other writers and with the marketplaces of literature: Edinburgh, Glasgow, London.

That may not be such a drawback as it appears. Even if it is a drawback, there are more than adequate compensations: for example, the imposing of a work-pattern without distraction, but — much more important — the possibility to see life as a harmonious whole. A place like Orkney is a microcosm of the inhabited globe; here meet and mingle most of the 'types' that compose the human race. They can be seen in all their shifting relationships and patterns; not only do we see the islanders who live and go about their various businesses, but we have knowledge of their roots in the past, we have stories (that quickly become legend) about their origins and ancestry and kin. There are some islanders — especially women — who have a detailed knowledge of the subtle complex web of kin of any person whose name crops up in any idle conversation. This delving into ancestry can, admittedly, be boring if it interrupts, as it frequently does, in the telling of an anecdote or piece of tasty gossip. But it is proof enough that a small community is not at all insular, a mere scattering of yokels and beachcombers. It is a rich and diverse entity: all of humanity reduced to a scale that can engage our sympathy, satire, imagination.

Looking at the great wheel of human life in a small segment is an ancient literary device. Chaucer chose a random company of pilgrims. James Joyce wandered about Europe but wrote entirely about the city he had exiled himself from, Dublin.

It happens that Orkney is an immensely rich quarry to draw upon. The islands have been continuously inhabited for five thousand years or more. The howes and tombs of the early nameless races lie scattered everywhere. A sophisticated and highly imaginative people built the stone circle of Brodgar, and Maeshowe. The remnants of stone keeps — 'brochs' — lie thick along the shores and loch-sides. The Picts left their stones with intriguing symbols carved on them. Then an invasion from the east broke over Orkney and the islands were strewn with a magnificent heritage of stories, *The Orkneyinga Saga*, and, most enduring of all, the 12th century Cathedral of St Magnus the Martyr in Kirkwall. That Norse period was Orkney's golden age. There followed a slow melancholy decline, marked by the infiltration of predatory Scots and the degradation of an independent farming community to the status of serfs and bondmen... There is a wonderful resilience about the human spirit. After the dark centuries, new characters appear in the landscape: lairds, ministers, land improvers, smugglers, witches, merchants and skippers. They fill our chronicles of the 18th and 19th centuries. Our own century has brought its own confrontation and challenges: two world wars which have changed the whole status and outlook of the islanders; the discovery of oil in the North Sea; the threat, so vivid a decade ago, of uranium mining. My novel, *Greenvoe*, deals tentatively with such threats.

Compulsory education, newspapers and books and radio and TV, have in the past century had an enormous influence on the life of the islanders. Orkney, with its maritime and trading links with Scandinavia and the Davis Straits and Hudson Bay, was never an isolated community – and there have over the centuries been continual infusions of new blood. The intrusions of technology, however, have diluted our identity too drastically.

Pollution, nuclear power, over-fishing, the continuing

destruction of the wild wet beautiful places, and the unique creatures that share our habitat, our fellow mortals: there are plenty of challenges for present-day islanders to face and resolve. Writers and artists ought to be in the forefront of the struggle.

For the reasons above, I count myself fortunate to live and work in such a place. If ever my pen goes dry, it will be for lack of energy or inspiration, never because the subject matter is exhausted. There is enough here to keep a whole school of writers going for the next century.

The three stories in this collection are random swatches from a huge web of possible subject matter.

I cannot offer, in all honesty, much comment on the art of the short story. The gift is innate and can't, I think, be learned from correspondence courses. What the story-teller must have is a feeling for rhythm and a sense of form or pattern. These are mysteries that lie at the heart of every art, music, dance, painting, sculpture, architecture, story-telling and poetry.

Without rhythm and pattern, nothing can be well made. Art — and by implication history and life itself — has, lacking them, no real meaning.

BERNARD MACLAVERTY

*R*emote

Around about the end of each month she would write a letter, but because it was December she used an old Christmas card, which she found at the bottom of the biscuit tin among her pension books. She stood dressed in her outdoor clothes on tiptoe at the bedroom window waiting for the bird-watcher's Land Rover to come over the top of the hill two miles away. When she saw it she dashed, slamming the door after her and running in her stiff-legged fashion down the lane on to the road. Her aim was to be walking, breathing normally, when the Land Rover would indicate and stop in the middle of the one-track road.

'Can I give you a lift?'

'Aye.'

She walked round the front of the shuddering engine and climbed up to sit on the split seat. Mushroom-coloured foam bulged from its crack. More often than not she had to kick things aside to make room for her feet. It was not the lift she would have chosen but it was all there was. He shoved the wobbling stick through the gears and she had to shout – each month the same thing.

'Where are you for?'

'The far side.'

'I'm always lucky just to catch you.'

He was dressed like one of those hitch-hikers, green khaki

jacket, cord trousers and laced-up mountain boots. His hair was long and unwashed and his beard divided into points like the teats of a goat.

'Are you going as far as the town this time?'

'Yes.'

'Will you drop me off?'

'Sure. Christmas shopping?'

'Aye, that'll be right.'

The road spun past, humping and squirming over peat bogs, the single track bulging at passing places – points which were marked by tall black and white posts to make them stand out against the landscape. Occasionally in the bog there were incisions, a black-brown colour, herring-boned with scars where peat had been cut.

'How's the birds doing?' she shouted.

'Fine. I've never had so many as this year.'

His accent was English and it surprised her that he had blackheads dotting his cheekbones and dirty hands.

'Twenty-two nesting pairs – so far.'

'That's nice.'

'Compared with sixteen last year.'

'What are they?'

He said what they were but she couldn't hear him properly. They joined the main road and were silent for a while. Then rounding a corner the bird-man suddenly applied the brakes. Two cars, facing in opposite directions, sat in the middle of the road, their drivers having a conversation. The bird-man muttered and steered round them, the Land Rover tilting as it mounted the verge.

'I'd like to see them try that in Birmingham.'

'Is that where you're from?'

He nodded.

'Why did you come to the island?'

'The birds.'

'Aye, I suppose there's not too many down there.'

He smiled and pointed to an open packet of Polo mints on the dashboard. She lifted them and saw that the top sweet was soiled, the relief letters almost black. She prised it out and gave it to him. The white one beneath she put in her mouth.

'Thanks,' she said.

'You born on the island?'

'City born and bred.' She snorted. 'I was lured here by a man forty-two years ago.'

'I never see him around.'

'I'm not surprised. He's dead this long time.' She cracked the ring of the mint between her teeth.

'I'm sorry.'

She chased the two crescents of mint around with her tongue.

'What did he do?'

'He drowned himself. In the loch.'

'I'm sorry, I didn't mean that.'

'On Christmas Day. He was mad in the skull – away with the fairies.'

There was a long pause in which he said again that he was sorry. Then he said, 'What I meant was – what did he do for a living?'

'What does it matter now?'

The bird-man shook his head and concentrated on the road ahead.

'He was a shepherd,' she said. Then a little later, 'He was the driver. There should always be one in the house who can drive.'

He let her off at the centre of the village and she had to walk the steep hill to the Post Office. She breathed through her mouth and took a rest halfway up, holding on to a small railing. Distances grew with age.

Inside she passed over her pension book, got her money and bought a first-class stamp. She waited until she was outside before she took the letter from her bag. She licked the stamp, stuck it on the envelope and dropped it in the letter box. Walking down the hill was easier.

She went to the Co-op to buy sugar and tea and porridge. The shop was strung with skimpy tinselled decorations and the music they were playing was Christmas hits – 'Rudolf' and 'I saw Mummy Kissing Santa Claus'. She only had a brief word with Elizabeth at the check-out because of the queue behind her. In the butcher's she bought herself a pork chop and some bacon. His bacon lasted longer than the packet stuff.

When she had her shopping finished she wondered what to do to pass the time. She could visit young Mary but if she did that she would have to talk. Not having enough things to say she felt awkward listening to the tick of the clock and the distant cries of sea birds. Chat was a thing you got out of the habit of when you were on your own all the time and, besides, Mary was shy. Instead she decided to buy a cup of tea in the café. And treat herself to an almond bun. She sat near the window where she could look out for the post van.

The café was warm and it, too, was decorated. Each time the door opened the hanging fronds of tinsel fluttered. On a tape somewhere carols were playing. Two children, sitting with their mother, were playing with a new toy car on the table-top. The cellophane wrapping had been discarded on the floor. They both imitated engine noises although only one of them was pushing it round the plates. The other sat waiting impatiently for his turn.

She looked away from them and stared into her tea. When they dredged him up on Boxing Day he had two car batteries tied to his wrists. He was nothing if not thorough. One of them had been taken from his own van parked by the loch shore and the thing had to be towed to the garage. If he had been a drinking man he could have been out getting drunk or fallen into bad company. But there was only the black depression. All that day the radio had been on to get rid of the dread.

When 'Silent Night' came on the tape and the children started to squabble over whose turn it was she did not wait to finish her tea but walked slowly to the edge of the village with her bag of shopping, now and again pausing to look over her shoulder. The scarlet of the post van caught her eye and she stood on the verge with her arm out. When she saw it was Stuart driving she smiled. He stopped the van and she ducked down to look in the window.

'Anything for me today?'

He leaned across to the basket of mail which occupied the

passenger seat position and began to rummage through the bundles of letters and cards held together with elastic bands.

'This job would be all right if it wasn't for bloody Christmas.' He paused at her single letter. 'Aye, there's just one.'

'Oh good. You might as well run me up, seeing as you're going that way.'

He sighed and looked over his shoulder at a row of houses.

'Wait for me round the corner.'

She nodded and walked on ahead while he made some deliveries. The lay-by was out of sight of the houses and she set her bag down to wait. Stuart seemed to take a long time. She looked down at the loch in the growing dark. The geese were returning for the night, filling the air with their squawking. They sounded like a dance-hall full of people laughing and enjoying themselves, heard from a distance on the night wind.

WILMA MURRAY

A House On Christmas Hill

'Martin, where are we going?'

'You'll see. It's not far now.'

'You said that ten minutes ago.' Kathy wrapped herself more tightly in her sulk in the front seat of the mini and concentrated on willing up a blizzard over the monochrome winter landscape.

They stopped at last on a farm track. With manic leaps and a lot of silly smiling, Martin led her to a gate, opened it and stepped aside with exaggerated courtesy to let her pass through.

'It's just a field,' she said.

'But not just any field. It's our field. Well, the firm's field. They've bought it to develop. What do you think?'

'What do you want me to say? It's a field.'

'But imagine it. We're going to build ten luxury houses here. See those trees? The pines on the rise with the snow on them? Doesn't it look a Christmas card? We're going to call it Christmas Hill. That was my idea, actually.'

'Well, well. But it's not a bit like a Christmas card. There's no coach and horses.'

'But do you like it?'

'Does it matter?'

'We could have a house up here some day. I have all the plans in the car. Come on.'

'Hey! Hold on ... 'But he was already gone, head in, backside out, rummaging in the back seat of the car.

He spread the plans out over the dashboard and steering wheel, talking non-stop, punctuating his speech with an insistent prodding finger. Kathy focussed only on his upper lip and let herself become slowly mesmerised by the sight of his teeth appearing and disappearing in some busy comic pursuit of their own. When she tired of that, she pretended she was a foreigner and had to struggle hard with his broad Scottish vowel sounds. None of it worked. She could still hear what he was saying.

'You can see it all already, can't you?' she said, without waiting for a gap in the flow of words.

'Of course I can.'

'Show me, then. Show me this house you'd like us to have.'

'This one. Look. The one on the corner at the top of the hill.'

'That's no good. I want to really see it. Now.'

'O.K. Get your scarf and gloves and come on.'

He ran to the top of the hill, his jeans white to the knees with powder dry snow. She followed more slowly, hunched in her coat and determined to be thoroughly miserable.

With a stick, he outlined the plan of the house on the fresh snow, counting steps for measurement. Then he began to draw in the rooms one by one, leaving gaps for doors.

'Stop!' he shouted at her as she threatened to wander into the plan. 'It's not finished.'

He piled so many words and images in front of her that she was forced at last to see the house. He leapt from room to room, describing and explaining, building walls out of his enthusiasm.

'It's done. You can come in now. But use the front door.'

'Georgian style, I presume,' she said. 'Two locks, a peephole and a chain on the inside. What are we afraid of, Martin?'

'It's a very secluded site. And we're rich.'

'My mini's going to look a bit out of place in the drive.'

'Oh, but we have a Range Rover now.'

She stood inside the space he had called the combo sitting room-dining room and looked around, assessing the decor.

'I don't like white walls. And there's no fireplace. I want a fireplace, with logs and real flames.'

'And a washhouse and an outside loo?'

'Lavvy. We say lavvy.'

'Not any more we don't.'

'I see.' She wandered into the kitchen space. 'What do you see me doing in here?'

'Oh, rustling up a great dinner for the boss and his wife or a steak for me on a Saturday night.'

'Give me the stick a minute.' She began to draw in some squares round the kitchen walls.

'What are you doing?'

'That's the cooker. And the sink and the table.'

'No, no. It'll be fitted. It's not going to be like the flat. Really, Kathy, you've no imagination.' He grabbed the stick back, rubbed her lines out with his foot and drew in his own vision in the snow.

'O.K. Have it your way.' She turned her back on him and walked into the bedroom, smiling. 'Martin! There's a man looking in at me from that house over there.' She pointed down the empty field. 'He's always watching me. He's the bank manager with the big Volvo and the leather golf bag. His wife keeps asking me over for coffee to show off the antiques she buys at country sales. Are you going to speak to him, Martin?'

'I'll punch his face in. Or. We could have our bedroom in the back of course.'

He followed her out into the back garden with this suggestion.

'Do we have a dog?' she asked.

'Yes.'

'Well, our dog's just shit on our next door neighbour's lawn. I'm hanging out the washing and she's giving me dirty looks. She's the retired schoolmistress, by the way. The one with the cats. Why don't you train the dog better, Martin?'

'That'll be your job. Anyway, you won't be hanging out the washing. You have a tumble drier. I told you. In the utility room.'

'O.K. So I'm pruning roses, then. We have lots of roses round the patio. Don't we, Martin? Well trained roses and a badly trained dog.'

'Kathy, stop this.'

'And are we letting our little Martin play with the American kids down the road? They're always in here, you know, asking for him and wolfing our cookies. But then you're never here, so you wouldn't know. But the parents are very liberated, so I hear. Whatever that means.'

'They probably hold fancy dress parties and have baths together.'

'You're getting the hang of this, Martin.'

'And you're showing yourself up.'

'Who to? Anyway, I don't like this house. It makes me unhappy. It makes me want to scream.'

'Don't you dare.'

'I will.' And she screamed three great ringing screams which carried across the field and hung locked in the cold air for what seemed like several minutes.

'For God's sake, Kathy.' He grabbed at her and she pulled away. 'Somebody might hear you.'

He grabbed at her again and they blundered around in an undignified struggle, obliterating all trace of his carefully drawn plan. She struggled free and stood panting white breath.

'See? Nobody came. I don't want to live in a house where nobody comes when I scream. And you're no damned use. You're only worried about what the neighbours will think. Well, they can think what they like. I'm leaving you.'

She ran then, leaping through the powdered snow, straight down the field and slammed into the mini's driving seat.

'I can't stay with you, Martin,' she shouted up at him as he came down the field to the car. 'I don't like the house and I hate the neighbours.'

'It doesn't have to be like that,' he said, leaning in the window of the car.

'You're bloody right, it doesn't.' She moved over into the passenger seat. 'Come on. Get in, you silly sod.'

DILYS ROSE

Magnolia

For Sale: Spacious ground floor flat. Central location.
Accommodation comprises living room, kitchen/
dining room, three bedrooms, bathroom with
shower. Ample storage. Extras.
Offers over £35,000.
For further particulars and arrangements to view,
apply to the subscribers with whom offers should
be lodged.

Grubb, Grace and Snell
Solicitors.

The tenement flat was set back a few feet from the pavement,
behind a flimsy fence and some earth. Puncturing the earth
were the stumps of rose bushes and a small leafless tree, a tree
occupying one corner of the plot between pavement and wall.
Late November. The earth hard. Nothing growing.

Inside it was everything they needed and more. They were
in no doubt that it was the best they had seen and put in an
offer as soon as they could contact their solicitor; a generous
offer, generous enough to secure the sale.

They moved in. It seemed empty, a little bare in comparison
to the cosy chaos of their previous flat which had, at the time
of occupation, been a continual poky clutter, more of a transit
camp than a home. Now there was so much space to inhabit.

They could stride through the hallway, stretch their arms wide and spin round without scraping their fingers against the walls. This was a place where they could stay for a while, take time to fix up just as they wanted, a place where they would repair the loose windowframes, the cracks in the plaster, a place where they could put down roots.

In the conditions of sale, the owners had made only one stipulation – that they could remove the tree from the patch of earth which was too small to be called a garden. Signing the deeds, the purchasers readily agreed. The tree was nothing special to look at, no more at that time of year than a few ordinary branches on a stunted trunk. Did it have sentimental value? Had the last people planted it when they first took on the place? They couldn't take it immediately, they said. Could they uproot it in the spring, after the flowering? Why not? the buyers instructed their solicitor and promptly forgot about the tree.

After a slow dark winter, spring finally arrived and the few feet of earth between wall and pavement responded. All the usual seasonal flora began to force its way through the hard earth — demure snowdrops, cheery crocuses, brazen daffs and tulips. The creeper crept further up the masonry and, a little later, the tree blossomed.

That was when they began to notice it, the tree which turned out to be a magnolia, rare in such northerly parts, a tree bending under the weight of its blooms like a bridesmaid sinking into a curtsey. By day its creamy pink petals unfolded, by night its heady scent drifted through the open window. A Southern Belle on a plain Scottish street.

During the days which followed, passers-by often stopped at the gate to admire the tree, to discover its name, to ask — if it wasn't being too cheeky — for a cutting. All the attention had the effect of increasing the householders' own interest. They began to take pride in the tree, observing it with the self-satisfaction of parents who had produced a beautiful daughter. They began to tend it, watering the roots regularly, inspecting the condition of the bark, the leaves, for blemishes and flaws about which they could worry and seek out remedies. The tree entered the routine of their lives. It entered their daydreams, transplanting them in distant, warmer climes. America. The Deep South.

One fine afternoon an elderly woman, leaning heavily on a stick, stopped at the gate. Her knot of grey hair, her bloodless complexion, clawlike hands were in shocking contrast to the vibrant tree she admired. When she didn't move on, the woman of the house, who was sunning herself on her doorstep, began to explain that the tree's occupation of her garden — she now felt justified in naming it so — was limited, that it was due to be dug up in the near future.

The stranger shifted her gaze from the tree to its keeper. With the far-off look of death in her eyes — the look of seeing beyond the gaudy garden, the sturdy figure of the householder, the solid walls of the tenement behind which the constructions of the city stretched for miles — she grieved over the fate of the magnolia.

'It may never bloom again,' she said. 'My peonies, I tore them from their beds. They didn't like it. They pine for familiar soil. It's the same with magnolias. I may not live to see my peonies bloom again.' She turned on her stick and continued along the street.

They have tightened window-frames, filled up cracks in the plaster. They have placed on mantelpieces, walls, shelves, windowledges, all their nicknacks, potted plants, books, mirrors, paintings. They have taken up every inch of the place with the trappings of their life together. They are allowing the dust to settle and are considering starting a family. They have grown accustomed to parting the curtains of an evening, gazing at the pale magnolia petals glowing in the moonlight as they listen to Billie Holiday singing of love and lynchings in the Deep South. They are at home. Home is a ground floor flat with a magnolia tree outside the living-room window. They have signed away their tree and now are loth to let it go. They have compiled a list of reasons to present — when the time comes — to the previous owners, reasons why the tree ought to remain in familiar soil, reasons quite independent of their own affection for it.

Meanwhile, the tree continues to put forth new blooms. Its roots push deep and wide, into the foundations of the house, under the pavement, taking up all the space they can find.

Snakes and Ladders

Lily picked at the hem of her coatsleeve while she waited. She was wearing her good coat today — at least, it used to be good but now it was fraying at the cuffs. Since Sammy went into hospital she had been losing weight and her clothes, as well as being shabby, drooped over her narrow shoulders. It didn't seem worth cooking a proper dinner just for one, and besides, skipping meals saved money. Not that there was ever any to save.

The waiting room smelled of disinfectant, like the hospital. The doctors there told her, when she could get hold of one, that Sammy was making 'some improvement' but she didn't notice any. The therapist said that Sammy was interested in clay and had him throwing fistfuls of it at the wall. Something about frustration, the therapist had said, but there was more to it than that. Everyone in her area must be frustrated if frustration meant throwing things. There were broken windows all over. Sammy would be normal if that was all there was to it. They were giving him drugs to 'regulate his behaviour'—that's what they said—but the drugs just made him talk a lot of nonsense or loll around with his mouth hanging open. He was like a lump of clay himself on those sedatives. He still screamed if anyone mentioned a cupboard. One day he threw *himself* at the wall.

'Number eight, please.' A thin woman got up, tugging at

the man next to her. He grunted, heaved to his feet and slouched after her through the door marked INTERVIEWS. The door clicked shut. Lily's plastic card had 9 on it so she would be next. She bit a ragnail and fixed her eyes on a poster directly opposite her. There was nothing else to look at. In black letters it commanded:

TAKE PRIDE IN YOUR ENVIRONMENT. DON'T SPOIL IT WITH LITTER.

The words were printed on a stretch of very green grass, sprinkled with daisies. Right in the middle of the meadow lay a pile of crisp packets and broken beer bottles. Who'd want to spoil such lovely grass? Lily couldn't remember seeing grass which looked as green. There was nothing in the poster which looked at all like Lily's area except the litter but even that looked wrong. You could sweep *that* up in a minute. Litter, as Lily knew it, meant streets of rotting filth which spewed out of drains every time it rained and crawled further and further up the walls of the flats. And the grass wasn't green, like that. It was nearer the colour of dishwater.

'Number nine, please.' The number eight people slammed the waiting room door behind them as they left. Lily went into the interview room, holding out her number. The young clerk coughed briskly into his fist. He scraped his chair forward until he was tucked in tightly behind his desk. He began thumbing through a pile of forms. Lily smiled, noticing that his shirt was missing a button. Needs looking after, she thought, just like Sammy.

'Now then. Your name is Marsh, Lily Marsh, is that correct?' The clerk spread his arms across the polished wood and leaned towards Lily. She nodded in reply.

'And you're divorced Mrs Marsh, am I right? And reside at 125 Hill View, 14B, Easter Drumbeath?'

'Yes.'

'And I understand you've applied for a transfer?'

'That's right. I want to move to another area.'

The clerk pulled a green form from the pile. It was a dull colour, a bit like the doors on the flats at her end of Hill View, where you couldn't see the hills. You could see the quarry though, a great lake of yellow mud. The council had repainted doors at the other end of the street a year past, but they'd stopped halfway.

'You see, my son's not well...He's in the hospital. He had a terrible shock...'

At that moment, the clerk was overwhelmed by a fit of sneezing.

'You should be in your bed,' said Lily. The clerk coughed then gave her a bleary smile.

'Yes I... no, I'm afraid some of us must keep going,' he replied, as though remembering a motto. He straightened up his papers.

'Now, can we go through this step by step, if you please.' He glanced at the clock while he spoke. 'You say your son resides with you.'

'He stays with me, yes. But we can't go on staying where we are.'

The clerk sighed, stubbed his pencil against the desk, took a deep breath.

'I'm aware that Easter Drumbeath is not the most desirable housing area but there's a long list for houses anywhere. Easter Drumbeath houses forty thousand tenants and I would say, at a modest estimate, twenty per cent of them have applied for a transfer within the last five years. Do you know how many people that is, Mrs Marsh? Eight thousand at least!'

'I know it's hard for other people in Drum. The place is in a terrible state. It's like ...' her fingers twisted into her cuffs, 'like the inside of a litter bin.'

'Ah, but you see, the council cannot be held responsible for litter. After all, who drops the litter?'

'It's not just that,' Lily began but the clerk still had his eye on the clock.

'I must explain to you that the council allocates rehousing through what we call a point system.' He raised his eyes to the ceiling as though he were trying to remember his lines. 'This is based on the present condition of the tenant's housing. I must emphasise that the waiting list is extremely long and, in all fairness, would be better closed for the time being. Even if your points do add up to the required number, it is likely to be a considerable time before the relocation takes place. With the situation as it is, it might be better not to raise people's hopes. Do you see what I mean, Mrs Marsh?'

The clerk peered at Lily with such weary eyes that she felt obliged to nod, although she wanted to ask about the point system and relocation and how long a 'considerable time' was likely to be. But she didn't want to be a nuisance.

'Let's start with you, Mrs Marsh. Do you work?'

'No.'

'What about your ex-husband. Does he provide any maintenance?'

Lily answered the first string of questions to the top of the clerk's head while he ticked off boxes on the green form.

'I have a note here to the effect that you are behind with your rent payments.'

'It's only three weeks behind,' she replied. 'It's the first time. You see, my son's in the hospital and the new payment scheme's not working properly yet.'

'There was a circular, Mrs Marsh, supplying advance information concerning the delay. You were advised to make alternative arrangements.'

Lily had received the letter but couldn't make alternative arrangements. She couldn't borrow money. Who was there to borrow from? No one she knew had money to spare and the pawn wouldn't give her anything for her belongings. The bus fares to the hospital. They added up.

'Still,' said the clerk, 'I imagine many people in Easter Drumbeath are in the same position. We'll try to find out what can be said in your favour, shall we? For instance, if you are lacking in some basic amenity, like a clean water supply, or electricity, it will be easier to push a transfer through.'

'They're going to cut off my electricity soon. I can't pay the bill.' Lily hadn't intended to mention the electric but the clerk seemed to be saying that having it cut off would help.

'I'm afraid that's no good, Mrs Marsh. If it had already been cut off, it might have made a difference but we can only take the present situation into consideration.'

'But the flats are damp,' said Lily. 'I've got to keep the fire on all the time. There's damp all over the walls, in big black patches.' The clerk took a note of this. The word "damp" was given a tick. One point to Lily. It was as if the two of them were playing a strange game of snakes and ladders, with Lily landing on more than her fair share of snakes. When the clerk reached the bottom of the third page of questions, there remained a small space without any boxes.

'Now, are there any particular circumstances you'd like to mention in the "Comments" section?'

Lily had been trying to tell the clerk about Sammy from the beginning and now there was just this little space left without any boxes.

'He had a breakdown, my son Sammy. He had a terrible shock and then he had a breakdown.' She paused. Would there be room for any more?

'Go on, Mrs Marsh.'

'There was this empty flat... on the floor below. Sammy used to go in there sometimes to ... just to look around, for something to do...' She couldn't say that he brought her floorboards for firewood. 'He was poking around, just looking at things. He'd told me about a funny smell coming from a cupboard. I said it would just be the damp because everything smells rotten when it's damp. The cupboard was locked. I said he shouldn't force it. I told him to leave well alone. But you know what kids are like. He got the door open. And there he was!'

'Who was, Mrs Marsh?'

'Mr Martin, from flat eleven, hanging from a rope, poor man. There were ... things moving all over him. Poor Sammy. Poor Mr Martin. I'm sorry!' Lily choked to a halt.

The young man was embarassed by the weeping woman in front of him but he had come across this kind of thing before. Sometimes it was just a put-on.

'So this ah... this breakdown you say your son had, this would have occurred as a result ... of the shock of seeing this ah... corpse?' Lily lowered her head. 'I do sympathise with you, Mrs Marsh. I'll try to do what I...' The clerk's condolences were cut short by another insuppressible sneeze.

*   *   *

Lily walked home along the canal. It was a long walk but it helped pass the time. It was a bright day and the sun stroked the back of her neck like a warm fingertip. Towards the end of the landscaped walkway, she began noticing the litter. A piece of broken bottle had trapped the sun on its curve and shone fiercely. A wisp of smoke curled round the jagged edge. Below the glass, the weeds were scorched.

She climbed through the torn fence where Easter Drumbeath's tangle of cement walkways snaked across the motorway. This was where the gardens abruptly came to an end, where the birdsong petered out. In Drumbeath the birds didn't stay long, except for the scavenging gulls: and they didn't sing, they squawked.

She glanced at the neat bungalows and their well-tended lawns. She'd always wanted a garden, a small one would do fine, a lawn set off with a blaze of colour in the flower beds. But they'd never give her a garden. On the path, the broken bottle had started a small fire. How easy that would be, she thought. She had heard of folk who'd done such things.

When she arrived at the centre, she counted out her change and stopped at one of the few shops which wasn't an off-licence or a betting shop. A row of fortresses, grilled and barred with iron. No one wanted a shop here anymore. The insurance was too high, the break-ins were too frequent, even with the iron bars and electronic alarms. She pushed open the heavy door.

The man behind the counter was filling in a pools coupon and smoking between coughs. On the counter lay a pile of shrivelled oranges next to slabs of sausage meat and discoloured bacon. The radio crackled out a song about the bright city lights of somewhere else.

'Yeah?' he said, without looking up.

'How much is a gallon of paraffin?' Lily asked, as casually as possible.

DILYS ROSE

*T*he Story of a Story

A Personal Essay

Where do you get your ideas from? How do you get published? How much money do you make? These are the three questions I am most frequently asked by students. As ideas come from every imaginable source, as publishing is an unpredictable business and payments range from the price of a fish supper to a small fortune, I'd like to tell you about just one story. I've chosen 'Snakes and Ladders' — included in this collection — as it was my first story to appear in print.

So where did it come from? Ideas seem to be elusive creatures. They appear at the most unexpected or inconvenient moments, like just before I fall asleep or when I am very busy with something else. The blank sheet of paper in the typewriter has a nasty habit of scaring them away. And ideas are unreliable. What initially seems like a good idea does not always make a good story. The idea does not fully develop until the story has been written. For example, the events in 'Snakes and Ladders' only formed into a clear *idea* when the story was complete. It began in an unspectacular way, as an image of a woman sitting in a café.

A few years ago, I worked as a cook in a community café on a large housing scheme on the outskirts of Edinburgh. Though the place was cheerful, this was in spite of circumstances rather than due to them. Many of the café customers had troubles which preoccupied them, isolated them. The woman who became the character of Lily Marsh started as no more than a face, a face and an attitude from that café. I did not know her real name or anything else about her. All I knew of her was what I saw, the way she sat at the table, sipping her tea. I called the woman Lily because I wanted the name to contain both what the character wanted from life — a clean attractive environment, a calm, sane life — and what she was experiencing at that time — substandard housing and incapacitating financial worries.

Some time later, I met a woman who worked as a health visitor. As I have always been inordinately fascinated by what people do to earn a living, I asked questions all evening. In some ways I was sorry I asked. I was made aware of more widespread deprivation that I had imagined in Scotland's capital. I took away from that evening one image — of an empty flat, its floorboards in flames.

I had a face, an attitude, a burning flat. It wasn't a lot to go on but I felt I had the beginnings of a story. The next element which I began to imagine was the interview. I had experience of unemployment offices and, though I did not remember any interview in detail, I remembered the sound of the clerk's voice, the mechanical drone of bureaucracy, the rehearsed impersonal response to need. At first, I had no idea how central this interview was going to be. I imagined that what happened when Lily bought the paraffin would be the central action. When I began to write, this scene became left unresolved — to suggest, amongst other things, that the game of chance would never really end.

A word about the setting: the story is set in an amalgam of real places. It was not intended to be a particular scheme, which is why it has an imaginary name.

What of the story once it was finished? I first sent it out to one of the producers of a radio programme called 'Morning Story.' It was politely rejected. I tossed the self-addressed envelope in the bin and went right off the story for a while! When I later took it out of the drawer again for a closer look, the story didn't seem too bad after all. I made a few amendments and sent it out again. This time it didn't come back. A politics/current affairs magazine published it. This was my first short story to be in print, and theirs. Since then, I'm pleased to say, the magazine has continued to publish a short story in each issue. I was pleased and terrified to see my story in print. It was out of my hands, in the world, with a life of its own.

Some time after, the story was chosen to be included in an anthology of women's writing, once we'd agreed on the name of the housing scheme! A letter came requesting that, as the place was clearly Drumchapel, a large housing scheme northwest of Glasgow, I should call it that and be done with it. Was there a street next to a quarry called Hill View in Drumchapel? Was there a canal which passed rows of neat bungalows before it crossed the motorway? Even if there *was*, I couldn't just change the name of the place. The details I included were put there to *be* part of the story, not to authenticate it. I held out for my fictitious name feeling that I had achieved something: to create a place which someone recognised, yet didn't exist. The next turn of events amused me at the time. Not long after the anthology was in the shops, another producer of 'Morning Story' telephoned me, saying that he'd read the story in the book and wanted to broadcast it! He had also checked the BBC files and seen the rejection slip. I agreed, with glee, that it be broadcast. There's an obvious moral here: if at first you don't succeed, hang about.

After the story had appeared in a magazine and a book, and been broadcast on radio, I assumed that would be its adventures over until I eventually wrote enough stories to put together in a book of my own. At that time, I had only a handful and so anticipated a long wait. Then the editor of a French magazine asked to translate it, and the editor of this collection decided to include it. This is the story of 'Snakes and Ladders' to date. Where will it go from here?

I Can Sing, Dance, Rollerskate

Cool in here. So cool and dark. This has gotta be it. I'll say: You gotta real nice place here, mister. Then I'll tell him. Why not? Hey mister, I'll say, I just walked all the way up First then all the way down Second, you know what it's like out there? I tell ya, it's hot. Not just regular hot but 98 degrees hot, you hear me? Heard it on the radio five times already. Five times, after the same bit of news about today's shooting in Brooklyn and this month's t.v. star overdosing on vitamins, the weatherman broke in to give us an update on the temperature. It's murder out there, mister, folks riot in this kinda heat.

Sure I look wilted, but I'm all set. Even brought a spare outfit, in case you don't go for classic black. Some folks find black depressing, funereal, I know it, but it don't show the dirt.

You know what it's like out there, I'll say: It's like the desert. There's a haze, a shimmer over everything. The whole of Manhattan looks like it's underwater, like it's dissolving into the smog. You don't walk through that heat, mister, you wade through it, slow mister, real slow, like a dream sequence in a bad movie. Today's been one hell of a bad movie, so far.

It's lonely out there, you know. Nobody's around. I mean nobody. The 'Walk, don't Walk' sign's been flashing off and on to no-one but me. The whole goddam city's deserted. But there's traffic, sure there's traffic, all heading the same way — outta town.

All the way up, all the way down for nothing, not even a 'maybe' outta fifty establishments. More. More like a hundred. I'll say: You know how far that is, you ever tried walking it? No, you'd take a cab. All the billboards would slide by, red lights would turn green, the blocks would just melt away. You'd take a cab but I walked, mister, from Third to Eighty-Eighth, from Eighty-Eighth back to Third, that's 85 twice — I can count good.

So maybe he heard the weather report already. So I'll tell him — sure it ain't the best day for it but I don't have a choice, see. Okay, so nobody in their right mind hangs out in the city today if they can help it, but that's my point, mister, *if*. See, I just got here from …no, I live here, mister, sure I do. Just got back from ..no, you won't know it. No sir, there's not a whole lot to know about where I got back from. So he wants to know where else I've worked in Manhattan. I'll say — okay I'll tell ya. I'll make a list. I can count and I can lie.

Even without the heat, I'd still get the flushes, the dizzy spells, the throwing up. Your symptoms are quite normal, Mrs Lemme. Positive, *Mrs* Lemme. Acting like we're all married. Simplifies their filing system maybe. Ain't that good? she says. No kidding, I call on the phone at five after nine for the results and that's what she says. So I'm putting her straight, giving her some background when she cuts in with: We don't require any personal details, Mrs Lemme, meaning she don't want no sob stories or mess on her doorstep. A termination comes around 300, she says, snappy as ever, like it was a bargain offer. But you gotta go outta town. The inner city list is way too long for you, Mrs Lemme. You should have contacted us a month ago. And I just got here.

Twelve hours it took to get here on the bus, sitting way back by the stinking john, stuck between two slobs, one with a cigar on the the go the whole way, the other with body odour. And the window jammed shut. Enough to make anyone sick. Twelve hours of going over potholes on the highway thinking, that one, that's done it. All it takes is a bump to get rid of it, a bump on the night bus. Some hope.

D'you wanna think about it? she says, meaning she ain't got all day to spend on me. Think about it? I ain't done nothing but. Watched all them women with kids go by past Marty's Grill, pushing their buggies up and down Main Street, piling groceries right in on top of their kids, hanging parcels on the handles of the carts. Every goddam one of them run down, worn out, sick of their dribbling screaming toddlers. You bet I've thought about it. Toddlers are tough but that's just the beginning. Of the end. Sixteen years plus. That's one hell of a pile of tips. When d'you need the cash? I wanna know before she hangs up on me. In advance, she says. For sure.

What's keeping this guy? Don't tell me, I'll say. I don't look fit enough to fix a milkshake, right? It's the heat, I tell ya. Why not step outside, mister, see what I mean, sample that atmosphere. There's no-one around, not even derelicts. Usually you're tripping over them, right? Usually they're like so many casualties strewn all over the sidewalk: guys with their legs in plaster, bag ladies with bandages instead of shoes, asleep or out of it. But not today. It's too hot even for them today. They've swarmed in Central Park. They're sprawling over a patch of shade. I don't blame them, mister. Just wait till you hear the news. There will be killings tonight.

So he wants to know why nobody hired me so far. Don't know what it was, I'll say, just bad luck, maybe. It happens. You'll know all about luck in the restaurant trade. Some days folks just don't wanna eat, right? Some days they only want what you just ran out of   you see, mister, I'll say, I'm familiar with the trade.

So he wants examples. No sweat. Take the seafood bar. I say to the guy: Okay, so I ain't never boned a fish for a customer — most folks can do it themselves. It can't be so hard. I can practise right now. By the time you open tonight, I'll be real slick. Gimme a whole tray of fish and I'll debone em right now. Na, na, na, he says, you gotta do it *at the table*. It's not *what* you do, it's how you do it. I need someone with showmanship, he says. So why not hire a showman? I say. He shows me out. At the noodle house they say: Sorry, gotta have black hair. Maybe you dye your hair, make up your eyes, come back next week. Next week I won't get into their uniforms. At the pizza joints, all ten of them, they shrug, point at their empty tables, tell me to come back in the fall. At the Jewish place they want me to sing, in Yiddish for Chrissakes, in between shifts. And I don't need to tell ya about the clubs — only body-builders in leotards get an interview.

Can I mix drinks, mister? Sure. Fix a wicked Bloody Mary, a lethal Godfather. How come nobody wants a waitress just to serve food around here?

Could have asked pa for a loan, but I wouldn't have got it, not without spilling the beans. I can lie, but not to pa, and the truth — he couldn't take it, not since ma ran off. Never forgave her for deserting him. Never forgave me my lack of ambition. Drop-outs disgust him. Deserters disgust him. He drives me crazy. He'd think I'd flipped. Coming all this way to get rid of it. Find me a shrink if he found out. Talks about the weight of responsibility like it was some kind of blessing. Some blessing.

I'm ambitious now. My own life in my own small, but not squalid, apartment — that's what I'm aiming at. Me plus a kid equals welfare, standing in line for handouts. And charity from pa. And that equals defeat. So many calculations. Had plenty time for calculations. Three hundred bucks — it ain't a lot around here. Coupla nights maybe, in the right place. This place has gotta be it. So cool and dark. A week. A week at the outside. Gotta be. A chance, I need a fast chance. And a drink of water.

Hell, Alma swung it for me. Not that she'd have encouraged me if she'd known. If she'd known I'd have got her schpiel about the sanctity of life and the rights of the unborn while we folded napkins. But maybe she guessed. Seven months gone herself and still shifting trays. Told her I was taking a vacation. She was happy. Needs all the overtime and tips available. Hasn't had a vacation in eight years, not since she hitched up with Prescott, the chronic student. Eight years of college fees to find and she a waitress on minimum wage. It'd make you cry. And in a nickel and dime joint like Marty's, Jesus. Prescott finally got wise when Alma showed him one of his own fertility graphs. Her chances of becoming a mother had gotten as slim as his own of ever finishing his research. She reckoned they'd better strike before the iron froze. Alma's smart — knows everything Prescott knows, and some. But Alma don't know what she wants.

I know no one wants me to keep it, not really. No one knows, not even Harry. He ain't been by in two months anyhow and, Jeez, if he got wind of it he'd cross the state line as fast as you can say gestation. Maybe that bitch at the clinic would like me to see it through. That way I'd make her job easier. One less termination to arrange. One less phone call.

I could sleep right now, it's so cool and dark. A week's work. Fire me after a week but it's gotta be now, can't come back next week. Next week's too late, heatwave or no heatwave. Can't think about it any longer. Each day it's harder to believe it can be got rid of, terminated. As if it's just a matter of flicking a switch, on, off, gone. Gotta be done before I start guessing at its gender. Before it's too late. Before I begin to picture a face. Before I can't face it.

You're my last stop, mister, I can't do this one more time. I'm getting lockjaw from this goddam smile. And my feet. Jesus. Not one more time today. Maybe tomorrow I'll go all the way up Third and all the way down Fourth. Maybe. But today this is the end of the line. Not another threshold, not another lobby, even a cool one like this. Not another, 'Hi, I'd like to speak with the manager'.

Positive, gotta act positive. Today's word. Today negative sounds a whole lot better. Gonna do it this time. Gonna say: Hi, I'm Joanne Lemme, Miss Joanne Lemme, experienced waitress, knowledge of steaks, seafood, Italian, Puerto Rican, Greek, Chinese, formal service, casual service, bar service, brisk service, service always with a smile. You name it, mister, I'll do it. I can sing, dance, rollerskate. My work record's clean as a fresh tablecloth. Anything you want. Gotta spare dress with me, but I'm average size, fit any uniform. Worked all over town. Sure thing. Just dropped in to check you out. Felt like a change, you know. Liked the look of your place. Real nice place you got here. I tell ya, I chose it. Said to myself, this looks like a fine place to work. There's no problem, mister, no problem. Thought you might be hiring, that's all. Thought you might have a start for a waitress. Lemme start tonight, mister, I'm all set. All I need's a glass of water. It's hot out there.

Any kids? he'll say. No, sir, no kids whatsoever.

*T*he Hunter of Dryburn

Yez'll have a drink.

Whit izzit, a pinta heavy izzit? A pinta heavy. N whitzzat yer young lady's drinkin? Hullo darlin, aaright? Aaright. Gin an tonic izzit? Gin an tonic it is. No problem friend, Ah insist. Pinta heavy na gin an tonic. On me.

Yez dinnae mind me talkin tae yez, dae yez? Mean dinnae get me wrong, ken whit Ah mean, Ah'm no meaning anythin or anythin. Mean Ah'm no tryin tae chat ye up or nuthn sweetheart. No tryin tae chat up yer burd or nuthn son, aaright son? Aaright. No me, naw.

Naw but is soon is yez walked through that door Ah could tell. Ah could tell yez were in love and that, the paira yez. Stauns oot a mile so it diz. Na could tell yez were educatit people ken. Na could tell yez wernae frae roon aboot here, that wiz obvious. See it's no very often Ah get the chance, mean tae talk tae folk like youz in here ken. Ah enjoy a bitty intelligent conversation ken. So Ah sez tae masel, whit wid the Auld Man adone? He's deid ken, death by misadventure. Yez probably read aboot it in the Evenin News. So Ah sez tae masel, the Auld Man widda bought these young people a drink, had a bitty conversation ken. See the Auld Man wis like that ken. Friendly. Hospitable pal, you've said it. Unless he didnae like the look o somebody, then he wisnae quite sae hospitable.

So yez took the wrong road frae the motorway, ended up in

sunny Dryburn? Jist thought yez might as well pop in for a quick wan, fair enough. Is soon is yez walked through that door Ah sez tae masel Aye, they've probly took the wrong road frae the motorway. Quite frankly like, if a thought for wan minute yez had come in here deliberately like, Adda tellt yez tae get yer heids looked. See Dryburn? Sa dump.

Tell ye this hen, you're beautiful so ye are. Naw seriously. Nae offence son, aaright? But Ah mean how diz a boy like you get a beautiful wummin like that? It beats me, so it diz. Nae offence son, aaright?

Aye Dryburn's a dump aaright. Mean yez can see that for yersels. Mean it's no whit ye'd caa a village even. Mean, whit is there? Thirz haufadizzen shoaps. Thirz a chip shoap. Thirz the church and thirz the chapel. An thirz four pubs. Five, if ye count the hotel up by the motorway. See folk used tae pass through here a loat before thon motorway. Nen there used tae be a station up by the steelworks. Thats where he worked, the Auld Man, afore he deed. Shut doon noo though, the steelworks. Yez widda liked tae meet the Auld Man, no that he went tae Uni or nuthn but. But he wis an educatit man ken, ayewis wi a book in his haund. Edgar Allan Poe, Ernest Hemingway, you name it. Ah've been readin a bitty this Ernest Hemingway masel ken, story boot shootna lion. Ken the wan Ah mean darlin? That's it son, that's the wan.

Aye he's a great writer right enuff. An thirz a helluva loata good advice aboot huntin an that in this story. Course it's aa aboot a place in Africa or somewhere like that, jungle an aa that ken, no a place like Dryburn. Whit's that yer sayin sweetheart? Aye it looks aaright frae the train right enuff, but sa dump. See the trains used tae stoap in Dryburn afore they shut doon the station ken. It used tae be mair o a community ken. A mean, no a community exactly but. But at least ye could get a train oot o the bliddy place. See the Auld Man wis a respectit person in Dryburn. Yez probly read aboot him gettin killt, in the Evenin News it wis. Aye. Mean he wisnae like a doakter or lawyer like, but folk looked up tae him ken cause he wis educatit. Educatit hissel so he did. Used tae sit in that coarner there, in his wheelchair ken, and poke folk wi his stick and tell them tae mind their effin langwitch. An folk pyed attention tae him tae. See everybiddy went tae him wi their payslips, Ah mean if they couldnae work oot their tax or their superan. Or like if somebody had tae go up tae court, they ayewis went tae him tae find oot their rights, ken. It wis like they consultit him aboot anythin like that. That's right sweetheart, you've said it: he wis a walkin Citizins Advice Bureau. Except he couldnae walk much ken, cause o his legs.

He had it up here see, the Auld Man, he could work things oot for folk. Take numbers for instance, he wis a wizard wi numbers. Mean if somebody had a win on the horses ken, the Auld Man could tell them exactly, doon tae the last haepenny, exactly how much they'd get back, minus the tax an everythin. Naebody could touch him at poker. Or dominoes. A wizard, he wis a wizard aaright. See noo that he'd deid there's naebody else like him left in Dryburn, naebody who can tell folk how much o a tax rebate tae expect ken. Except mibbe me. See that's why Ah've startit tryin tae educate masel a bit ken, that's why Ah'm talkin tae youz educatit folk like, so Ah can mibbe learn somethin frae yez.

Tell ye somethin son, ye're bloody lucky so ye are. Beautiful wummin like her, don't try an deny it.

So Ah'm readin this Ernest Hemingway tae try and educate masel a bit ken. See me and the Auld Man used tae go in for a bit o huntin wirsels, up by the Union Canal. Course, there's no very much tae hunt roon aboot here. Nae lions an tigers, ken? But there's a helluva loata rats up there at the canal. Hundredsa big dirty great rats. Ah wonder if Ernest Hemingway widda done the same, Ah mean if he lived in this area. No much else tae dae in Dryburn except hunt rats, take ma word for it. Mibbe he'da enjoyed it, ken, then he'da come in here wi me an the Auld Man efter a guid night's huntin an had a few pints wi us. Aye, right enuff son, it wid be Absinthe if he wis buying. Here that wid gie Louis, the barman owre there, that wid gie him somethin tae think aboot. Absinthe by goad. See Louis used tae take a rise ootae us when we came in here wi the guns ken. 'Here come the big game hunters!' he'd say, or: 'Bag any tigers the night boys?' He wis ayewis at us aboot it ken, then wan night the Auld Man shot him. Yez shooda seen Louis' face. Yez shooda heard the langwitch in here that night! Ah mean he wisnae hurt or nuthn, the pellet jist nicked his airm. Course, the Auld Man said it wis an accident ken, said he wis jist pretending tae take aim ken an the thing went oaf in his haund. Yez shooda heard Louis, talk aboot wild! He wis gonnae bar the baith o us, but he needed the custom ken. Louis stoaped pullin oor leg aboot it efter that, Ah can tell ye.

Ever shot anything son? Naw? Ye dinnae agree wi it? So how come ye like readin Ernest Hemingway, eh?

Skip it son.

Ah gave it up anywey, efter the Auld Man deed. See that's how he goat killt in the end. Yez musta seen it in the News, quite a scandal so it wis. Well, we were up there oan the canal bank wan night, ken, jist sittin watchin the ither bank. It wis near the railway bridge up there, ken? Yez've probly seen the canal frae the train. That's where ye get the rats. So there we were, me an the Auld Man, jist waitin, when who should come along but two well-known members of the local constabulary, ken?

Mean Ah ken it's no nice, shootin rats, it's no very nice, but if ye've read Ernest Hemingway ye'll ken aa aboot the waitin bit. It wis the waitin bit that wis guid — like fishin, ken? Nuthin in the canal tae fish for though, that's why we got the guns in the first place. We didnae talk much, me an the Auld Man, when we were waitin for the rats. Naw, we jist liked sittin there oan a nice night, wi the sun oan the water an aa that, waitin. So along came this pair and startit askin us questions an aa that. The Auld Man jist sat there sayin nuthin, so Ah did the same. See, he wisnae a very talkative person unless he felt like talkin, an he never really liked talkin tae the polis. He widnae say somethin unless he had somethin tae say, see whit Ah mean? Aye, you've said it son, laconic. The Auld Man was laconic as hell sometimes. An this was gettin up the polis's nose, the wan who wis asking aboot the guns and what not. Nen the ither wan says, An what exactly is it ye're plannin tae shoot in any case? Nen the Auld Man says: Vermin. Jist like that, Vermin. Oh, so it's vermin, is it? says the first wan, the wan askin aa the questions, an then he says somethin aboot us bein vermin wirsels. Nen it transpires they want us tae haund owre the guns there an then. See it wis when wan o them tried tae take ma gun that it startit. A fight. Now, can Ah ask ya tae tell me, honestly, do Ah look like a violent person? Do Ah, tell me straight? Naw, Ah'm no violent. Well, hardly ever. But it wis like when ye're wee, in the playground at schuil, an somebody bigger than ye tries tae take away yer luck-bag, ken? That's whit it wis like — Ah jist saw red. So there wis a bitty a scuffle oan the canal bank, ma gun went oaf an wan o them got a pellet in the neck. Then the coshes, ken? Ah wis strugglin wi baith o them when Ah realised the Auld Man wis in the canal. He'd went right under. Probly he tried tae get in among us wi his stick, ken? An he musta got pushed intae the water. Ye can imagine whit it wis like. Ah couldnae swim tae save masel, neither could the Auld Man. So the wan withoot the pellet in his neck had tae strip oaf an dive in. Ah remember the ither wan sayin, Let the auld bastard drown! By the time we got him back up oan the bank, he wis deed. So that wis that.

A tragedy, the paper called it. Course, Ah wis up in court for resistin arrest, assault an aa the rest o it, but the judge wis lenient cause o the Auld Man an that. Whitzat hen? Ring a bell, does it? Think ye mibbe saw it in the News? Aye, it's likely.

Sorry tae be sae morbid an that.

Thing is, Dryburn's no the same place withoot the Auld Man. Ah blame masel for whit happened. Ah shoulda had mair sense than tae start a scrap wi the polis. So Ah'm tryin tae educate masel, see, so Ah'll be able tae help folk decode their pyeslips an that.

Tell me somethin before ye go, friend. What's yer honest opinion o Ernest Hemingway as a writer? A ken he's a great writer an aa that, but earlier the night Ah wis readin that story aboot shootn the lion, and Ah donnno. Ah couldnae be bothert feenishin it. Ah came doon here for a coupla pints insteed. It's no Hemingway's fault ken, it's ma fault. Ah wis enjoying the story an everythin, till it gets tae the bit aboot the kill ken. Cause the trouble is ye see, Ah jist cannae imagine the lion. Ah jist cannae picture the lion in my mind, know whit Ah mean? Aa Ah can imagine's a rat, a dirty hairy great rat. A rat's no the same thing as a lion, somehow.

Yez'll be on yer way, then. See, it's no very often Ah get the chance tae talk tae educatit people like youz. Ah wisnae tryin tae chat ye up or nuthn sweetheart, aaright? Aaright son? Ah wisnae tryin tae get aff wi yer burd or nuthin son. See Hemingway? See if he did live in this area, in Dryburn like, he'da probly left years ago an got hissel a joab as a journalist.

Ah'll tell ye somethin else while yer lady friend goes tae the toilet, son. It's no very often we get wummin like her in here. Nae offence, but she's quite a catch. Quite a catch, Ah'm saying. If ye want ma advice, haud ontae her. Or somebody else might, believe you me.

Ah'm no meanin anythin or anythin, but ye're a jammy wee swine so ye are and don't you try an deny it.

Kreativ Riting

'Today, we are going to do some writing,' said PK. 'Some *creative* writing. You do know what I mean by *creative*, Joe, don't you?' he said to me.

'Eh ... is that like when ye use they fancy letters and that?' I said.

'No, Joe, it is not. Creative writing has nothing whatsoever to do with they fancy letters and that,' said PK. So I made the face, like Neanderthal Man, and went, 'UHHH.'

We call him PK 'cause his name is Pitcairn, and he is a nut. So anyway, he goes round and gave everybody a new jotter each.

'For God's sake now,' says PK, 'try and use a bit of imagination!' Then he stops at my desk and looks at me and says, 'If you've got one, I mean. You have got an imagination, Joe, haven't you?'

This is him slaggin' me, ken?

So I says, 'Naw, sir, but I've got a video.'

That got a laugh, ken?

So then PK says, 'The only trouble with you, Joe, is your head is choc-a-bloc with those videos and those video nasties. Those video nasties are worse than anything for your brain, Joe.'

Then Lenny Turnbull, who sits behind me and who is a poser, says: 'What brain? Joe's no got a brain in there, sir, just a bitty fresh air between his lugs!'

That got a laugh, ken?

So I turned round and gave Lenny Turnbull a boot in the leg, then he karati-chopped me in the neck, so I slapped him across his puss for him.

PK went spare, ken.

Except, naebody took any notice, so he kept on shouting: 'That's *enough* of that! Come on now 4F, let's have a bit of order round here!'

So then I says, 'Sir, they video nasties is no as bad as glue is for your brain but, is it?'

That got a laugh, ken.

Then Lenny Turnbull who is a poser says, 'Joe's got brain damage, sir, through sniffin' too much glue!'

'Glue sniffing ... solvent abuse is no laughing matter, let's have a bit of *order round here*! Right. I'm going to get you all to do a piece of writing. You've got a whole two periods to do it in, and what I'd like all of you to do is empty your mind. In your case, Joe,' he said to me, 'that shouldn't be too difficult.'

This is PK slaggin' me again, ken.

So I says, for a laugh, ken: 'How no, sir? I thought you said my mind was choc-a-bloc with video nasties?'

That got a great laugh, ken.

So then PK says, 'That's right, Joe, and what I want you to do is just empty all that junk out of your mind, so that your mind is completely blank, so that you've got a blank page in your mind, just like the one in your jotter. Understand?'

'But sir, this jotter's no blank — it's got lines in it,' I says.

Then PK says: 'Joe, your head probably has lines in it too, through watching all those video nasties.'

Everybody laughed at that, so I did the face like Neanderthal Man again and started hitting my skull with my fist.

'UHHH! UHHH!'

'Joe,' said PK, 'I knew you'd hit the headlines one day.'

Nobody laughed at that though, so PK said: 'You're a slow lot today, aren't you?' So I did the face again. 'UHHH!'

'Right,' said PK, 'as I was saying before I was so rudely interrupted, what I want you to do is to empty out your mind. It's a bit like meditating —'

'What's meditating?' said Podge Grogan, who sits beside me, 'is that like deep-sea diving or somethin'?'

'Not quite,' said PK.

'Of course it's no!', says Lenny Poser Turnbull. 'Deep-sea diving!'

'Well,' said Podge Grogan, 'It coulda been! That's what it sounds like — deep-sea divin' in the Mediterranean Sea and that.'

'Aye!' I says, 'Deep-sea meditating — that's right, I've heard o that!'

'Away ye go!' says Lenny Turnbull, 'Deep-sea meditatin! Yez are off yer heids, you two!'

'Meditating,' says PK, 'as far as I know, has nothing to do with deep-sea diving at all, although, when you think about it, the two activities could be compared. You could say that meditating and deep-sea diving are … similar.'

So me an Podge Grogan turned round in our seats and looked at Lenny Turnbull.

'See?' says Podge, 'Deep-sea meditatin'. Tellt ye.'

'They're no the same at aw!' says Lenny Turnbull. 'Ah mean, ye dinnae need a harpoon tae meditate and that!'

'Ye dae in the Mediterranean!' says Podge.

'Aye,' I says, 'sharks and that. 'Course ye need a harpoon!'

'Aye,' says Lenny Turnbull, 'but you're talkin aboot deep-sea divin' — no meditation'!'

'Well, Lenny', says PK, 'maybe you could tell the class what meditating is.'

'It's what they Buddhist monks dae.'

'Yes, but how do they do it?'

'They sit wi their legs crossed and chant an aw that.'

'Well …' says PK, 'yes, but —'

'Naw they dinnae,' says Podge Grogan, ''cause Ah've seen them. They dance aboot an shake wee bells tegither and sing Harry Krishner, that's how they dae it!'

'That's different,' says Larry Turnbull, 'that's no them meditatin', eh no, sir?'

'Well, no, I don't think so … in any case, there are different ways of meditating, but basically, what you have to do is to empty out your mind. You'll find that it's harder to do than you think. Your mind will keep thinking of things, all the little things we clutter our minds with every day —'

'How's that like deep-sea divin'?' says Lenny Turnbull.

'Well … it's hard to explain, Lenny,' says PK, 'I just meant that when you meditate you sort of dive into the depths of your mind. And that's what I want you to do. If you're lucky, you'll find something down there. Some treasure. A pearl.'

'Dae we get tae use harpoons?' says Podge Grogan.

'No, pens.'

'Awwww!' everybody says.

'Now listen,' says PK. 'It's quite simple really. All I want you to do is write in your jotter whatever floats into your mind. I don't want you to think about it too much, just let it flow. Okay?'

'OK, PK!'

'Anything at all. It doesn't have to be a story. It doesn't have to be a poem. It doesn't have to be anything. Just whatever comes into your heads when you've emptied your minds. Just let your mind *open up*, *open up* and let the words *flow* from your subconscious mind, through your pens into your jotters. It's called 'automatic writing' and you're lucky to have a teacher like me who lets you do automatic writing, expecially first two periods on a Wednesday.'

This is still PK talkin', ken?

Then he says, 'I don't want you even to worry about punctuation or grammar or anything like that, just let your imagination roam free — not that you worry about punctuation anyway, you lot!'

So I says for a laugh, ken, 'What's punk-tuition, sir, is that like *learnin'* tae be a punk?'

Then everybody groaned.

'Joe,' says PK, 'will you just *shut up*.'

So I says for a laugh, ken, 'Hear that? First he's tellin' us tae *open up*, and now he's tellin' us tae *shut up*!'

That got a brilliant laugh that.

Lenny Turnbull (poser) said, 'But sir, what if nothin' comes into yer heid when ye're sittin' there wi yer pen at the ready?'

'Anyway,' I says, 'how can I write anyway, 'cause I've no got a pen anyway?'

'Use yer harpoon!' says Lenny Turnbull.

'You can borrow this pen,' says PK, 'but it's more than this pen you'll need to write, Joe, because to write you also need inspiration.'

'What's that?' says Podge Grogan, 'a new flavour o chewing-gum?'

So I burst out laughin'. PK went spare again.

Then he brings this cassette out of his briefcase and says, 'Right, I want you to listen to this piece of music I've got here, so that it might give you some inspiration to get you going. Just listen to the music, empty your mind, and write down whatever comes out of the music into your heads. Okay?'

'OK, PK!'

'What is it, sir? Is it 'The Clash'?'

'No,' says PK, 'It is none of that Clash trash. That Clash trash is even worse for your brain than video nasties *or* glue, Joe.'

Everybody laughed. So I did the face. 'UHHH.'

'If the wind changes, your face might stay that way,' says PK.

'Right, now stop wasting time. The music you're about to hear is not 'The Clash' but a great piece of classical music by Johann Sebastian Bach.'

'Who's she?' says Podge Grogan.

'*He*,' says Pk, 'was a musical genius who wrote *real* music, the likes of which you lot have probably never heard before and probably won't know how to appreciate even when you do. Now, I want you to be quiet and listen very carefully to this wonderful classical piece of music and just let go, *let go* and write absolutely anything the music makes you think and feel about. It is called, 'Air on a G string'.'

'Hair on a g-string?' I says.

Everybody fell about, ken?

'Come on now 4F, let's have a bit of order round here!'

Then Lenny Turnbull says, 'But sir, can we write *absolutely* anything we want, even swearin' and that?'

'Absolutely *anything* you want to,' says PK. 'Just listen to the music and *let go*. I promise no member of staff will see it, except me. If you don't want me to read it, I won't. The choice is yours. You can either read out what you've written to the class or you can give it to me and it will be destroyed. Okay?'

'OK, PK!'

Then Lenny Turnbull said, 'But sir, what about sex and that — can we put sex in it as well?'

'Hold on a minute,' says PK.

So I says for a laugh, ken, 'Hear that? First he's tellin' us to *let go*, and now he's tellin' us to *hold on*!'

That got a laugh, ken.

PK started clenching his fists, so the knuckles went all white, and he glared at me and his face went beetroot like he was going to go spare at me again.

'Look here, you lot,' says PK, 'we haven't got all day. You've wasted nearly a whole period already with your carry on and I am sick to the back teeth of having to RAISE MY VOICE IN HERE IN ORDER TO MAKE MYSELF *HEARD*! Will you please sit *still*, keep your hands *on* the *desk* and *you*, Joe Murdoch, are asking for *trouble*! One more wise crack out of you and you will be out that *door* and along to the *rector*, is that *clear*?'

'Yup.'

'As I was saying, you may write anything you like, but I don't think this piece of music will make you think about sex, because it is not an obscene bit of music at all. In fact, it is one of the most soothing pieces of music I know, so *shut up* and *listen*!'

So then Pk gets the cassette machine out of the cupboard where it is kept locked up in case it walks, and he plugs it in and plays us this music. Everybody sits there and yawns.

Then Podge Grogan says, 'Sir, I've heard this afore!'

'Aye, so've I!' everybody starts saying. Then Lenny Turnbull says: 'Aye, it's that tune on the advert for they Hamlet cigars!'

So then everybody starts smoking their pens like cigars and PK switches off the music.

'Put your pens down!' says PK. 'Any more of this and I'm going to give you a punishment exercise and keep you in over the break! I am aware that this music has been used in an advertisement, but that is not the point of it at all. The point is, it was written centuries ago and it has survived even till today, so *belt up and listen to it.'*

So we all sat there and yawned till the music was finished, but nobody got any inspiration out of it to write anything at all.

So then PK says: 'If anybody is stuck, you could always write something or other about yourself. Describe yourself as others see you. 'Myself as Others See me'. Now I've got a pile of prelims to mark, so I want you to keep quiet and get on with it.'

So here it is. This is my kreativ, automatic, deep-sea meditating writing:

MY OWN SELF AS OTHERS SEE ME

MY NAME IS JOE MURDOCH AND I AM SHEER MENTAL SO WATCH OUT. I HAVE GOT A GREEN MOHAWK. IT HAS GOT SCARLET SPIKES. ON MY FOREHEAD I HAVE GOT A SKULL AND CROSSBONES. ON MY BLACK LEATHER JACKET I HAVE GOT 200 CHROME STUDS NOT COUNTING THE STUDS ON MY BELT AND MY DOG COLLAR. ON MY NECK I HAVE GOT A TATTOO IT SAYS CUT ALONG THE DOTTED LINE. ON MY BACK I HAVE GOT NO FUTURE. ON MY BOOTS I HAVE GOT NO HOPE. IN MY POCKET I HAVE GOT NO MONEY. MY MUM LOVES ME AND I LOVE HER BACK. MY DAD STOLE THE LEAD OFF OF THE DALKEITH EPISCOPALIAN CHURCH ROOF AND I GAVE HIM A HAND AND WE DIDN'T GET CAUGHT. I AM A WARRIOR AND I AM SHEER MENTAL SO WATCH OUT OK. THE END.

And now I will take it out to PK and tell him I don't want to read it out to the class, and I don't want him to read it either. I will tell him I want it to be *destroyed*. That should get a laugh, ken?

F*ollow On*

Silver Linings

Before Reading

● Discuss in groups what you would do in each of these situations:

1 You find a £1.00 coin on a shop floor, next to the cash desk.
2 You find that someone has left a cassette of Mozart's greatest hits in the supermarket trolley which you are about to use.
3 You discover, having left the shop, that the assistant has given you change out of £10.00, instead of the £5.00 which you gave. The assistant is a friend, you have known her for years.
4 You find a £20.00 note in your school corridor.
5 Your parents have just bought from a friend a second-hand wardrobe for your bedroom. In it you find a small compartment containing £1,000 in old notes.

During Reading

● Stop reading at the sentence: 'We extracted from the lining of the coat £1,010 in old bank notes!' Discuss in small groups what you think *should* or *will happen next*.

After Reading

● In small groups discuss possible answers to the questions below. (One person should act as *group leader* and should ensure that everyone contributes and is listened to by the others. One person should act as *group reporter*. He/she should record the main points of agreement *after* each question has been fully discussed and be prepared to report some or all of these back to the class.)

1 Some short story writers use a 'hook' to draw us into the story and keep us interested. What is the hook that Joan Lingard uses in this story? At which point in the story did you first become aware of it?
2 Some short stories focus on a *debate* or *issue*: a problem which makes us think, what would *I* have done in this situation? What is the debate in this story? What would you have done if you were Sam or Seb?
3 Short story writers have a limited space in which to show us

what people are like. Draw up a list like the one below and find a sentence (or sentences) in the story which shows us most clearly what these people are really like. The first one is done for you. Then, try to number them in order of their importance in the story.

People	Sentences	Importance
Granny	She tints her hair auburn and is employed as manageress at a local supermarket.	
Father		
Mother		
Samantha		
Sebastian		
Morag		

4 How does Samantha's granny see others in the family? Try to find evidence in the story to support what you say.
5 'Morag and I helped haul in the catch.' Do you think this expression is a good one to use? Why?
6 'Well, I don't know. Maybe legally, but morally ... I mean, I suppose I should give it back.' Find who says this. Try to describe in your own words what the difference between 'Legally' and 'Morally' is.
7 Who is telling the story? Why does Joan Lingard not tell the story herself? Is there any advantage in having a character, who is involved, tell us the story?
8 Discuss the ending of 'Silver Linings'. Did you find it a good one? Can you suggest other possible endings? Why would your ending be better?

Options

In small groups

● You and a friend find a £20.00 note in the school corridor. You keep it. Your parents find it in your school bag. Role play the situation at home that evening.

On your own or in a small group

● 'Every cloud has a silver lining.' Joan Lingard's story is based on an old *proverb* or saying which is supposed to contain some wisdom. Try writing your own story based on some other proverb, altering them if you wish. Here are some more to think about. Discuss those in groups or with your teacher.

— Money doesn't grow on trees.
— Don't count your chickens before they are hatched.
— Between the Devil and the deep blue sea.
— Charity begins at home.
— Truth will out.
— All that glitters is not gold.
— It is better to travel with hope than to arrive.

On your own

'My granny isn't one of those grandmothers who sits and knits in the chimney corner, shrouded in shawls, if such grannies exist at all.'

● Write personally about what your grandmother, or grandfather, is *really* like, OR about what she/he *should* be like. Remember SUPER GRAN?

On your own or in a group

'She's for Beauty without Cruelty. As I am myself.'
' "Poor animal," said my mother.'

● Do some research into 'Beauty without Cruelty' and other similar groups. Try to find addresses and write to these groups for information. What do you think of Animal Liberation?

● Write an article for your school or local newspaper, or script a talk for your group under the title:
                    Animals — Their Right to Life
You could adopt this structure or devise one of your own:

The problem — Animals are being denied a natural life.
The facts
Views of people interviewed
Conclusion: your own views, based on fact *and* opinion.

• Imagine that 'Silver Linings' is the first chapter of a new novel. Write the second chapter, developing the story in a new way. For example, Samantha's father re-discovers the coat... End your chapter in such a way that your reader will want to read Chapter 3...

A Time to Dance

Before Reading

• In large groups, discuss your own or someone else's experience of 'skiving' — playing truant.

Where did you go, what happened when you returned to school and why did you do it?
Suggest some reasons why students may deliberately stay away from school. Try to work out what 'school phobia' is.

During Reading

• Stop at the sentence, 'They took the number twelve to St John the Baptist's'. Nelson has been caught skiving by his mother. Having finished work, she's now taking him back to school. With a partner or on your own, try to *predict* what will happen to Nelson there.

After Reading

• In small groups discuss possible answers to these questions: (Remember to decide on a *group leader* and a *reporter*. Each person should be aware of what he/she has to do.)

1 Why does Nelson play truant?
2 What do we learn about his and his mother's background?
3 What does his mother do to earn money?
4 What is your opinion of Mrs Skelly as a mother?
5 Do you have any feelings of sympathy for Nelson, or do you see him as a thoughtless, lazy boy?
6a Why do you think Bernard MacLaverty makes so many references to the eyepatch throughout the story?
6b Read the last sentence of the story. Why do you think the writer chose to finish his story at this point?
7 *Mood.* This story is about a boy who has no friends, he's a loner, a lonely figure who has very little to look forward to. Yet it's not all sadness. Try to find examples of humour, say which you liked best, and try to say why the writer has *mixed* humour, sympathy and sadness in this way.
8 Why do you think Bernard MacLaverty chose 'A Time to Dance' as the title for his story?

9   Finally, make a list of things which still puzzle you about the story, or of things which you find confusing or vague.
10   If the writer were to visit your class and ask you what you thought of his story, what would your response be?

Options A

On your own or in pairs

'As he left, Nelson noticed that his mother had put her knee up against the Housemaster's desk and was swaying back in her chair, as she took out another cigarette.
    "Bye, love,' she said'.

● Mrs Skelly is now alone with Mr MacDermot. After reading again their conversation up to this point, CREATE AN EXTRA SCENE in which the two continue their conversation. What do you think they would discuss? Try to reveal something of their different personalities through what they *say* to each other.

On your own

● Imagine that Mrs Skelly sits down that evening to write a letter to her sister in Ireland. She honestly tells about Nelson, his school and her own job. She pours out her true feelings and asks her sister for advice. Write her letter.

● You can feel lonely even when you are in a crowd of people. Write personally about a time in your life when you felt alone although lots of people, even your friends, were nearby. Concentrate on your *feelings* and on the actions of others. You could begin like this:

…I sat down. They stared at me as if I were mist, a vapour. They didn't smile…

On your own or in a group

● Write a *story* or script a *play*, or *role-play* scenes about skiving/ truanting. It could be in four sections or scenes:

    the decision
    the freedom
    the discovery
    the outcome

but not necessarily in this order! You could use 'Time Out' as a working title until you think of a better one. You could record or video your play and/or read your stories dramatically on tape or VCR.

On your own

'I'm going to try to be better from now on'. (Nelson)

• Write about a promise *made* which you have or have *not kept*. It could be a promise to yourself!

MORE STUDENTS TAKE TIME OUT

DO SCHOOLS BREED SKIVERS OR IS SOCIETY TO BLAME?

This Week's Investigative Report By …

• You are the ace feature writer working for the local newspaper. Mrs Joan Turner, chairman of a School Board, has telephoned your Editor to say that truancy in local schools is increasing and that she is determined to do something about it. The Editor wants *you* to write the feature article: you have been given the job of researching the facts, interviewing people, getting near the truth of truancy and giving *your* opinion. You've already drafted a rough plan. Here it is:

Outline the problem: Truancy claimed to be on the increase…
Outline the facts: Truancy rate now 6% more than 1980.
　　Only in High Schools, no increase in Primary Schools!
　　Fewer attendance officers now than in 1980…
　　Unemployment in local area has increased by 3%
　　Part-time jobs done by teenagers under 16: an increase.
　　Increase in the number of working mothers and single-parent families.
Views of people interviewed: report on interviews with:
　　one Head Teacher
　　one parent
　　two students.
Conclusion: Why is truancy on the increase? Blame society, schools or students. What can be done in the future?

Now write your article.

Anima

Before Reading

• In large groups share your experiences and opinions on one or both of these topics.

　　Talk about the most embarrassing experience which you can remember from your own childhood, or someone else's.
　　If you weren't yourself, *who* would you most like to be? Or, if it's easier, discuss *what* you would most like to be.

After Reading

• In small groups discuss possible answers to these questions:

1 'Hurry up and make up yer mind' is the first sentence in the story. At which point in the story did you first realise what the boy had to make up his mind about? Why does Brian McCabe not make it all clear to us at the beginning?

2 Why does his sister decide to dress him up as a girl? Do you think what she does is helpful, funny, insensitive or cruel?

3a Try to explain what this sentence near the end of the story means to you:
   'No, the girl in the mirror was smiling *at herself*, pleased to see herself at last, smiling in triumph.'

3b The last sentence of the story is extremely long. Read it again carefully, discuss and decide whether or not you find it effective as a concluding sentence.

4 Try to find and write down all the references to 'seeds' in the story. Say *what* eventually happens to the seeds and *why* the references to them may be important.

5 *Animus* — the masculine principle present in the female unconscious.
   Anima — the feminine principle present in the male unconscious.
   Say whether you find these dictionary definitions helpful in understanding the title of the story. Do these help you to understand the story itself better?

6 The *theme* of a short story is the *idea* or message which the writer wishes to illuminate for us, the readers. Some writers often highlight more than one theme in a story. Some students have said that these are the themes within 'Anima':
   Making decisions
   Freedom of choice
   Personal identity
   Being what you are, not what others want
   Stereotyping
   Do you agree with them? If so, list these themes in order of their importance in the story, leaving out some and/or adding more of your own.

7 From whose *point of view* do we see the events which take place?
   the father?
   the sister?
   the boy?
   the writer as a boy telling the story?
   the writer as an adult remembering the story?

8 Try to describe your personal reaction to 'Anima'. Did you find it funny? sad? disturbing? Did it make you think? Say whether something in the story still puzzles, confuses, or

irritates you.

9 Now read Brian McCabe's personal commentary on his writing and on how he came to write 'Anima' in particular. You may wish to read another story, 'The Full Moon'. If so, can you see any similarities of theme or technique?

Options

On your own

● If you've enjoyed reading 'Anima' and you've discussed it fully, write a critical evaluation of the story for your coursework folio. Guidelines for this are printed later in the Follow On section.

'What to be. How could I decide what to be?'

● Write personally about the decisions you have already made in your life or still have to make.

● Write a poem called 'Me, by Me.'

In a group

● Script or roleplay the scene at home as you are getting ready for the *most* important party in your life. Perhaps it's your first one — or last! Make the mood humorous *or* threatening.

On your own or in pairs

● Later that night the boy's father and mother talk about what happened. Script or role-play the dialogue. You could record it for play-back to your class later.

On your own or in a group

'(Faint? Wasn't that what girls were supposed to do?)'
'(Screaming? But wasn't that what girls ...?)'

● *Think*: What *are* girls or boys supposed to do?
     What *are* the roles which you are expected or not expected to play in your life?
Research: find out about gender stereotyping and sexism.
Interview adults to find out if attitudes have changed.
Present your *ideas, facts and opinions* in writing for your coursework folio *or* in a talk to your groups/class *or* as a debating speech *or* as a video documentary.
Use, if you wish, one of these as a working title:

Roles People Play
Mums and Dads

What Did *You* Do In The Great War, Mummy?
Janet and John are Miners
Who Am I?

On your own

• Read Brian McCabe's personal commentary again, especially where he describes how images develop in his mind. Now write your story around the woman on the bridge, or around an image of your own, making 'every event, every image, every word *count*'.

The Full Moon

After Reading/Listening Once

• In large groups work out:

1 Why was the writer working in the hospital?
2 Who or what did the American visitors think he was?
3 What does Billy seem to realise?

After Reading Again

In small groups discuss these questions:

1 Brian McCabe, writing about his other story 'Anima', has said:
   'The theme of the story ... has something to do with personal   identity, ... and how people define each other'
   Do you think that this applies to 'The Full Moon' too? Consider:
   How have the Americans 'defined' the writer?
   How has the writer 'defined' the Americans?
   How has the writer 'defined' Billy in the past?
   What happens to alter his view of Billy?
2 The full moon has often been associated with madness.
   Find as many references to the moon as you can throughout the story and show how the writer has *extended* this association: for example, what do the two sides of the moon represent?
3 Why do you think the writer chose to end the story as he speaks to Billy? Which *accent* will Billy use when he says, 'What is it?'
4 If you were to be labelled, mistakenly, as mentally ill, what would *your* reaction be?
5 Which labels have other people pinned on you? Do these 'define' you accurately?

Options

On your own

• Try to recreate the thoughts which may have passed through Billy's head as he watched the writer's embarrassment.

• Try to place yourself, through your imagination or your experience of others, in the shoes of a handicapped person. Write about a day in your life, in prose or poetry, when you suddenly become aware of how others see you.

• Do people 'label' you according to your family; friends; clothes; opinions; looks; intelligence; abilities; accent; job ...?

• Write personally in prose or poetry under the title

PACKAGED AND LABELLED

• Plan and write your own story called 'Mistaken Identity'.

• Plan and write a comparative evaluation of 'The Full Moon' and 'Anima' for your folio, concentrating on how the theme of identity has been illuminated for you.

Secrets

After Reading

• You may find that some things in the story still puzzle you. In your group or with your teacher discuss:

1 Why does the boy secretly read his Aunt Mary's letters?
2 What does he find out about John?
3 What does he find out about Brother Benignus?
4 Why does he cry that his Aunt 'might forgive him'?

• Now read the story again. Working on your own or in pairs, try to think about and write your responses to these topics:
1 The title of the story is 'Secrets'. What is Aunt Mary's secret? What is the boy's secret? Why does each not wish to reveal their secret?
2 The story is structured in four sections. How old is the boy in Sections 1 and 4? How old is he in Sections 2 and 3?
3 What happens in each of the four sections, in brief, is that:

Aunt Mary is dying.

118

Aunt Mary tells the boy not to read the letters.
The boy secretly reads her letters.
His mother clears up after Aunt Mary's death.

Obviously there is a flashback or time shift here. However, there are other references in the story to *times past* and to the future — what *may* happen. Try to find and list as many of these references as you can. How many generations might the story refer to?

4   How much do you learn about these relationships?

The boy/young man and his girlfriend.
The boy/young man and his Great Aunt Mary.
The mother and Aunt Mary.
Mary and John.

Which relationship features most importantly in the story?

5   The boy's *father* is never mentioned. Why do you think the writer has left out this character?

6   Find evidence which suggests what kind of house the boy lived in. What does this show about his family's background and life style?

7   Irises, Aunt Mary's flowers, are referred to in sections one and two. Which differences can you see in these references? In section one, what is the effect of the writer's use of the words 'scrolling' and 'clearing up'?

8   Why do you think that Aunt Mary's favourite extract, because she read it so often to the boy, was 'Pip's meeting with Miss Havisham from *Great Expectations*'? Why is this both sad and ironic?

9   Why was John able to write such long, detailed and sensitive letters to Mary during the war?

10 'The room could then be his study'.
She took off the elastic band and put it to one side with the useful things and began dealing the envelopes into the fire'.
Try to say what effect these sentences had on you, in the light of what you have learned about the people in the story.

11 Read the last paragraph again. Try to say what effect it is intended to have on you, the reader.

12 Bernard MacLaverty's story shows an extraordinary depth of feeling and has much to say about
Forgiveness and not being Forgiven
Love and Disappointment
Death and the Continuation of Life
Communication and Silence

Would you normally expect to find so much in a short story? Which, for you, is the most important THEME?

Options

On your own

● Write your own story in which someone has an *unrevealed* secret, *discovers* a secret or in which two people *share* a secret. Work out the *structure* carefully before you start. You may wish to structure it round a time shift.

On your own or in a group

'I watched him choke and then drown in his blood.'

● Find and read Wilfred Owen's poem 'Dulce et decorum est' or 'Exposure', and other poems written during/about the first world war.

● Try to research into conditions experienced by both soldiers and civilians during the Second World War.

● Try to write a series of letters (uncensored) between a soldier/conscript and loved one/relative at home which will evoke the love and the difficulties felt by both.

On your own or in pairs

'I am full of anger which has no direction'.
'I must do something, must sacrifice something to make up for the horror.'

● Research into the conditions under which soldiers/civilians existed in

The Korean war,
Vietnam/Cambodian war,
The Falklands war,

or exist in

Northern Ireland,
the Middle East,
Nicaragua,

or are involved in 'Trouble Spots.'

● Imagine that you are a soldier or civilian caught up in the horror of a military or guerrilla war. Write a letter, like John in 'Secrets,' expressing the horror and your real feelings.

● Write a poem under any of these titles: Anger, Sacrifice, or Horror. (You could also think about prisoners of conscience and write to

Amnesty International for information. Read *Talking in Whispers* by James Watson.)

On your own

'I love you as much as ever — more so that we cannot be together.'

• Build up a love story through extracts from letters which ends in either disappointment or happiness for one of the writers.

'He cried … that she might forgive him…'

• Write a short story, dramatic scene or poem based on the idea of forgiveness.

• Imaginative response: try to continue Bernard MacLaverty's story from this point:

'…His mother placed the poker on the hearth. She touched his arm. "Why are you crying …?" The boy reveals his secret, what he had done as a child. All his *feelings* pour out.'

• Write a critical evaluation of 'Secrets' for your coursework folio. See Guidelines, p. 139.

Silver

After One Reading

• 'Silver', as the writer has said, is 'a rather sad little story of a boy's disillusionment: the first hurt that love gives him'.* The boy's quest for Anna is narrated in a series of six short 'scenes'.
In a small group try to list briefly what happens in each scene. The first is done for you.

1 The boy sets out for Muckle Glebe with innocence, hope and a gift.
2
3
4
5
6

• Now read the story again. In small groups, discuss and record your responses to these questions:

1 Who is narrating the story?
2 How old is the boy?

3a Try to describe the boy's personality and background.

b Try to describe Anna's personality, background and history.

c Show clearly the contrast between her and the boy.

4 The skipper says at the beginning of the story, 'You'll never get her'. Why does the boy seem to think that he will succeed in his quest for Anna?

5 On his journey he trades two of his three gifts for information. What information does he get in return? Why doesn't he accept it as TRUTH?

6a What piece of information signals the end of the boy's quest?

b Do you feel sorry for him? Why?

c '...a jagged skeleton'. Why do you think these words might be appropriate to end the story?

7 Throughout the story the writer builds up a series of CONTRASTS or OPPOSITIONS.
Make a list of these:

  Shyness and …
  Youth and …
  Poverty and …
  Hope and …
  Lies and …

What do you think these contrasts contribute to the story?

8 The title 'Silver' could refer to three things. Try to work out what these could be.

9 There are two 'Chains' mentioned in the story. Try to work out precisely how these are related and what happens to both.

10 The writer's *style* is in keeping with the narrator and the setting. How would you describe his style and say why you feel that it is appropriate.

11 Do you think the boy was really in love with Anna or with an illusion? Is love an illusion?

Options

In pairs

• When the boy returns to the 'Kestrel', the skipper is keen to know if his prediction was correct. Script their conversation then read it to your group.

On your own

• George Mackay Brown has said, 'I feel that this boy wasn't a *negative* character, he had a certain style — what they call in Aberdeenshire "Smeddum" — and somebody in the not too distant future he will find a love which is rare and rich as gold'.*

Write a story, again narrated by the boy, now older, about his successful quest for love.

● Write a story, this time with Anna as narrator, beginning when she returns to the island, her engagement broken.

● Write a story or a poem using one of these titles:

The Gift
Unwelcome Truth
Love is for Night and Stars
There Must Be Love Songs

The Wireless Set

Before Reading

● Find out (1) what *propaganda* is and (2) who William Joyce, 'Lord Haw-Haw' was.

After Reading The Story Carefully

● In pairs or on your own, record your answers to these questions;

1   Where has Howie returned from?
2   Why does he feel it's right to introduce the wireless to Tronvik?
3   Even in Section 1, we find that the wireless utters what is useless and incorrect. Find and record some examples.
4   In Section 2, why does Howie have to leave Tronvik?
5   Why does the wireless then become the centre of attraction?
6a Find and list as many examples of propaganda as you can.
b   Lord Haw-Haw was responsible for some of it. How was Betsy able to prove that he was 'The father of lies'?
c   'He had a kind of *bestial joviality* about him'. Try to explain this apparent contradiction.
7   The tone of Section 2 is both sad and humorous. List or quote examples of both.
8   Read the last paragraph of Section 2 again then show how the writer contrasts the reality within the Eunson household with the unreality of the world outside it.
9   What has happened to Howie?
10 Why does Betsy seem to reject the 'sympathy' of Mr Sinclair, the missionary?
11 Why does Hugh destroy the wireless set?
12 Mr Sinclair is 'awed by such callousness'. Why don't Hugh

* Source acknowledgement: BBC Radio Scotland.

and Betsy even mention Howie? Do you too think that they *are* callous?

Options

• Write a letter to Hugh and Betsy who, you feel, deserve sympathy. Explain why you are writing, why you sympathise with them, what they could have done to change events, but why life has to go on.

• George Mackay Brown's novel *'Greenvoe'* dramatically portrays the impact of an alien culture on a timeless island community. Try reading the novel.

• Move on to the Extended Assignment, Truth and the Media.

Andrina

During Reading

• Stop reading at 'I was utterly bewildered' — the end of section two. Try to PREDICT what may happen in the final section of the story.

After Reading Once

• Try to work out who 'Andrina' *is*.

After Reading Again

• In pairs, record your answers to these questions:

1 Who is narrating this story?
2 Do you think that the STYLE is appropriate to the narrator? Why?
3 'She did not come again on the third afternoon'.
   Why is this sentence by itself in a solitary paragraph?
4 'Love had been killed but many ghosts had been awakened' 'A ghost appeal'.
   Show how the writer has prepared us for the ending of the story.
5 'I imagined ... Captain Scott writing his last few words in the Antarctic tent'. Why, at this point in the story, should the narrator imagine this?
6 Try to show how the writer has built up a sense of expectancy and longing throughout the story.
7 Words like 'lamp', 'ministrations', 'peace' and 'pure' help

build up a picture of Andrina in the old man's mind. What does he perceive her as?

8a In section two there is a story within a story. Try to summarise the old man's tale in your own words.

b At what time of year does his tale take place? Show how this contrasts with the time setting of the main story.

c Why do you think he narrates the tale to us, his listeners?

9 At what time of year does the final section begin? Why do you think this might be significant?

10 Try to work out what the last paragraph means for the skipper and for us, the readers of his story.

Options

On your own

• Imagine that Captain Torvald, the skipper, replies to the letter from Australia. Write his letter.

• Stanley the postman and Isaac the landlord meet in Tina Stewart's Post Office. They discuss Captain Torvald — his past and present. Script their conversation.

• Try to plan and write a short story of your own, which, like 'Andrina', combines two genres. For example:

Romance   Science Fiction
Supernatural   Thriller
Whodunnit   Historical

• Plan and write a story of your own in which all is revealed at the end by means of a letter. (You may wish to compare the use of letters in Bernard MacLaverty's story 'Secrets'.)

• Read George Mackay Brown's personal reflections on 'The Art of Narrative', p. 67. Firstly in small groups, then in your own essay, discuss the rhythm, form and pattern of the three stories represented in this collection or of any others by the same writer.

• How do 'Silver' and 'Andrina' compare with typical Romance stories?
In a group, do a survey of romantic fiction in your school or local library — Mills and Boon, Sweet Dreams, Historical Romance, popular magazines — and try to find out if there are common elements:

Happy endings
Character stereotypes
Plot conventions

Try to use (or send up!) one or more of these elements in a piece of Romance fiction written by *you*.

• 'But there was a sense of desolation on me'. Captain Torvald's loneliness arises out of what happened in the past and Andrina's apparent disappearance. Now read and compare 'Remote' by Bernard MacLaverty in which a woman is placed in similar circumstances of desolation.

Remote

Before Reading

• Read or listen to 'Andrina' by George MacKay Brown, then discuss the source and reasons for the loneliness which the old man experiences. Does he overcome his sense of desolation?

After Reading Once

• Find evidence in the story which determines how old the woman is.

• To whom does she write the letter? Why does she write it?

After Reading Again

• Here are a number of short extracts from the story. In small groups find where these occur in the story and say how each helps to illuminate the situation of the central character;

1   'Around about the end of each month she would write a letter, but because it was December she used an old Christmas card.'
    'On Christmas Day. He was mad in the skull ...'
    'When they dredged him up on Boxing Day he had two car batteries tied to his wrists.'
    'When "Silent Night" came on the tape ...she walked slowly to the edge of the village.'
2   'Twenty-two nesting pairs — so far!'
    'They sounded like a dance hall full of people laughing and enjoying themselves, heard from a distance on the night wind.'
3   ' "Where are you for?"
    "The far side!" '
4   '...points which are marked by tall black and white posts to make them stand out against the landscape.'
    '...the top sweet was soiled, the relief letters almost black ... the white one she put in her mouth.'

- A feature of the writer's craft is his use of finely observed *detail*. For example:

    'Mushroom-coloured foam bulged from its crack.'

Find other examples of the writer having used his pen as a camera. What do those details contribute to the story?

- Explain why you think 'Remote' is, or is not, a good title.

Options

On your own

- Imagine what the woman *may* have written in her letters, either before December or on this anniversary of her husband's death. Would she write to herself or to him or to whom? Try to write the letter.

In pairs

- Stuart, the postman, knows what's going on. He is a practical but sympathetic man. Imagine that he tells his wife about the monthly encounter and record their conversation.

On your own

- Loneliness is the central theme of this story, as it was to a certain extent in 'A Time to Dance' and 'Andrina'. Write an essay which compares how this theme is presented by the writer in two of these stories.

- You can feel lonely in a crowd of people, for many reasons. You can feel lonely in your own home, surrounded by familiar things. Plan and write a story in which the central character is revealed as desolate, an outsider. Does anything happen to change this?

- Now move on to the Guidelines section printed later which considers creative writing in your coursework folio.

A House on Christmas Hill

Magnolia

Before Reading

On your own draw a bird's-eye view of the house in which you live, like an architect's drawing — only not so precise. Then write brief responses to these questions:

1 Who designed your house?
2 What would you like to change about its design?
3 What would have been different if the house had in fact been designed by your mother or father?

• In mixed-sex groups discuss and produce plans for the perfect house.

• Read the two stories and discuss in small groups.
A House on Christmas Hill:
   1 Martin and Kathy are the two characters. Describe the *mood* of each.
   2 What does each seem to consider as more important when 'discussing' their future home?
   3 Which of the two, Martin or Kathy, do you most sympathise with? Explain why you do so.
   4 Would you like to live on Christmas Hill? Explain why/why not.
   5 Would you describe this incident as
         an argument?
         a silly game?
         a power game?
         a battle of the sexes?
      Find evidence to support your assertion.
   6 Who wins in the end? Say why you think so.
Magnolia:

   1 Do you think it was a good idea to begin this story with an advertisement?
   2 Show how the sentence structure in paragraph one echoes that use in the advertisement, and how it also provides a subtle *contrast*.
   3 What does the new house offer the new occupiers?
      What does it lack to begin with?
   4 Dilys Rose has said that the 'main character' in this story is the tree! Try to say why this is so.
   5 Another character is the elderly woman. What do you think was the writer's purpose in introducing her into the story?
   6 Comment on the significance of the last paragraph.
A House on Christmas Hill and Magnolia:

   1 Contrast the use of *dialogue* in both stories.
   2 Imagine that Kathy and Martin are the unnamed characters in 'Magnolia'. Which of the two stories would then be first in a *sequence* of stories about their life together? Suggest what a third story in the sequence might be about.

Options

On your own

• Assume that 'Christmas Hill' is the first chapter of a novel. Discuss ideas first, then write all or part of Chapter 2 which is set in a flat, and in which the characters of Kathy and Martin are developed further.

• The owners of the Magnolia tree return to claim it. Continue the story from this point, or script the conversation which will ensue. Clearly reveal the people's feelings towards the tree and what it means to them.

In pairs

• A *symbol* is an object which stands for or signifies something else, usually an abstract idea or emotion. Conventionally accepted symbols include the Cross, signifying the Christian religion, and the flag, which symbolises a nation, or patriotism.
What do these symbolise: a dove, the moon, a red rose, a skull? In 'Magnolia' the tree could be said to symbolise the growth and new life of a family. Try to plan and write a story which like 'Magnolia', focuses on a central symbol. You could use a tree or a wave, a bird, an apple, sunset, a window, or a road. The road (or railway) has been a symbol — of loneliness and rootless drifting — in many films.

On your own

• Rewrite 'Magnolia' as a poem.

• Write a personal reflection called 'Roots' in which you describe your feelings about your home, the people who share it with you; your neighbourhood and the neighbours who live there. What influence have these had on you?

• If you completed the 'Before Reading' section, write a journalistic essay, or illustrated magazine article on:

House Design — Built for Robots, by Robots   *or*
Who Needs Architects?

In pairs

• Write the estate agent's advertising material for the new luxury homes on Christmas Hill, *and* for the sale of *your own* house, making it seem as attractive as possible. Look at how estate agents do this, and include drawings or photographs which will show the houses to best advantage.

Remember—you can't make claims which are dishonest!

In groups

● Devise a board game to reflect both the excitement and the problems when buying/selling/renting/moving house. It could be called 'It's your move' and you could use a variation on the Snakes and Ladders format.
If successful — market your game!

● Now read Dilys Rose's story, 'Snakes and Ladders'.

Snakes and Ladders

After Reading

● Move on to read the writer's personal reflection called 'The Story of a Story', in which she says 'The game of chance would never really end.'

On your own

● Continue the story from where Lily throws the dice — or, possibly, the match.

In pairs

● Extract the dialogue from the story and read it dramatically as a straight interview, one person taking the part of the clerk, another the part of Lily.

In groups of five or six

● Write the script for (read and record) an extended Radio 4 report on 'The Housing Crisis in Easter Drumbeath'. It could follow this sequence:

1   A review of housing conditions by the reporter/ presenter.
2   An interview with a resident, perhaps Mrs Martin.
3   A report on Mrs Marsh's case.
4   An interview with a social worker, Mrs White, on why Mrs Marsh deserves sympathy and what she can/can't do to improve her circumstances.
5   An interview with Mr Clark, a local councillor.
6   An interview with the press officer of a national pressure group such as Shelter.
7   Reporter/presenter's conclusions; need for urgent action — but what action can be taken?

On your own

● Dilys Rose's story is based on an interview and on the idea of a child's game — Snakes and Ladders — only the game is more tragic than entertaining. Write your own story which focuses on an interview situation in which people do not really communicate, for example a job interview or a parent-teacher 'consultation'. (You could read about the interview between Billy and his Careers Officer in Barry Hines' novel 'A Kestrel for a Knave'.)

• Write your own story which is based on a more sinister version of a child's game, or on a situation where you feel that chance holds all the useful cards.

I Can Sing, Dance, Rollerskate

The Hunter of Dryburn

Before Reading

• Two volunteers should pre-read these stories and rehearse for dramatic reading to the whole group.

After Listening/Reading

• In groups. Both stories are MONOLOGUES, 'speeches' uttered by the main character. Consider ONE or BOTH stories and after discussion, write notes in response to these questions:

1 Who is talking to whom?
2 Is the accent authentic — in keeping with the setting?
  Does the accent help *establish* the setting?
3 What does the speaker reveal about his/her own character and the character/opinions of others?
4 What do we learn about the speaker's circumstances?
5 What is the *mood* of the speaker? Do you feel sympathetic towards him/her? Why/why not?
6 Which *themes* or issues arise out of what has been said? Say how you personally react to these issues.
7 Consider whether the writer has used other devices to illustrate the themes: eg. contrast, highlighting significant details, a significant final sentence.
8 Say whether you thought that the monologue form was effective in revealing character, situation and theme in this story.

• Now on your own expand and redraft your ideas/notes into a personal evaluation of one story or a comparison of both for your classwork folio.

Options

In groups

• In which situations would the MONOLOGUE be an effective and realistic form for a short story? Consider:

A boy/girl/teacher outside the Headteacher's door rehearses what she/he will say.
A man/woman speaks to an answering machine.
A little girl speaks to her teddy bear.

Try to make up a list of at least three more situations. Then, on your own, use one of those to write your short story in monologue form. Remember to use an accent, if appropriate. When finished, present your story to your group or class.

You could record some of the most interesting or unusual stories for a tape programme called 'Voices'. You could even send it off to the BBC or local radio.

In groups or as a class

• Be prepared to persuade others of your point of view, or prepare for a debate on:

1   The rights of the unborn child come first — abortion must be banned.
2   Unwanted pregnancy means unwanted children — abortion should be available on demand.
3   The National Health Service should always be free to all.
4   People who can afford it should pay for health care.
5   The working class no longer exists; there is only the unemployed and the rich.

EXTENDED ASSIGNMENTS

Oral History

'We have stories (that quickly become legend) about their origins and ancestry and kin' — George Mackay Brown.

● People thrive on stories, even the reliable press is a collection of news *stories*. Many older people have memories rich in anecdotes which will never appear in print. Ask an elderly relative or friend if you can interview them about their memories. Give him/her an outline of the questions you may ask and say that you would like to hear old stories too. The questions could be about:

Roots: e.g. Where did your family come from?
Memories of Childhood: What was the house like that you lived in as a child? What did you play at when you were young?
Memories of Schooldays: What are your happy or unhappy recollections?
Memories of World War Two: (Some people may not wish to talk about this.)
Memories of: A Working Life; Relatives who were unusual/famous; Stories heard and passed down through generations

Come back after some time to conduct the interview.
Make notes AFTER, not during the conversation; writing or taping puts people off.
Bring back and present to your class or group any interesting material and/or stories which you have heard. This could be built up into an ORAL HISTORY RESOURCE.
The people you have interviewed may never be able to write down their memories, so you could do it for them and indeed *give* it to them. A preserved memoir or story can be as treasured as a photograph.

Images of Scotland

Discuss in groups

● The stories in this collection are set in diverse places — Edinburgh, Dryburn, Easter Drumbeath, the Orkney Islands and far beyond. Do the stories convey any impression of Scotland as a 'Nation'? Or is your impression one of rootless people drifting across a scarred landscape?

How do *you* see 'Scotland'? Research into the images of Scotland which have been portrayed on film and on TV. Consider the kilted Scot who eats haggis and simultaneously plays the bagpipes. Does this stereotype still exist, or has it been replaced by others?

In groups

• Draw up a list of items which you feel contribute to Scotland's positive and negative image in the eyes of those who live within and beyond its boundaries. Then, decide what should be done to alter the negative image. Write an *article*, for a Scottish magazine, called 'A Nation Once Again?'.

• You could do the same for your own region, county, town, village, street, or even school. Then make a *video documentary* which shows the good, the bad and the ugly with a voice-over commentary.

• Prepare for a *debate* on '*Image* is more important than *reality*'.

• Prepare and present an exhibition of images, prose and poetry which will reflect the future image of Scotland (or of your area).

Story into Film

In groups

• Discuss which story in this collection could be made into a half-hour play or film for television. Bernard MacLaverty's 'More Than Just the Disease' is one possibility. 'Silver Linings' by Joan Lingard could provide episode one of a series about Sam and Seb — or a soap opera set in a slightly impoverished but trendy area. WestEnders?

• Write a letter to a senior producer at the BBC or ITV/Channel 4 in which you recommend that a short story be adapted for television. Say:

The title, author and publisher of the story.
What the story is 'about'.
What the writer's purpose was.
Why it should make a good film.
Which audience would be more likely to watch it, what they
   might find interesting or appealing and why.

Give advice on *setting* and where the film could be shot in order to create '*atmosphere*'.
Suggest which *scenes* the TV screenplay could concentrate on, leave out, or expand.

Suggest whether the story's *ending* should be retained or changed.
Give advice on *casting* the leading actor/actress: what should he/she
be able to portray?
Now, you could file your letter in your coursework folder or, you
could — and should — *send* it. You never know what could happen.
Ask your teacher for names and addresses.
If you have a video camera, do the storyboard, write the screenplay,
organise the cast and props and film it yourselves. Then send the
video to Channel 4!

Truth and the Media

Background Reading/Viewing

'The Wireless Set', George MacKay Brown.
'The Veldt', Ray Bradbury.
'The Pedestrian', Ray Bradbury.
'1984', George Orwell (a horrifying account of how power in a
totalitarian society is maintained by the media which defines 'truth'
for its people.)

Discuss in a group

• What are your reactions to some of these statements?

'This wireless speaks the truth'.
'Men speak, but it's hard to know sometimes whether what they
say is truth or lies'.
'The first casualty in war is truth'.
'I believe that in the end the truth will conquer'.
'The object of oratory alone is not truth but persuasion'.
'The truth shall make you free'.
'Two and two make five'.

• It has been suggested that man has never actually set foot on the
moon, that the whole gripping, heroic story was filmed in Holly-
wood or on secret location in America. Consider: how do you *know*
that Neil Armstrong was the first man on the moon?

Topic: The Presentation of 'Truth' by the Media

Research A

• Look up the television schedules for one particular day. Work out
the time allocated to fictional programmes (serials/films/comedy,
etc.) and factual programmes (news/documentary/sports report-
ing). How much time was allocated to each? Was this typical of other
days? Do you think the *balance* was correct?

135

• Study carefully one NEWS programme, say, 'The Six O'Clock News' or 'News at Ten'. List and count the total number of news items (stories) and record the time devoted to each one. Which was the lead story? How and why was it given prominence? Who decided that it was the most important? Did *you* think it was more important than the other stories? If not, say which other item you would have featured.

• Concentrate on the lead story. Calculate approximately how much time was devoted to giving the audience:

Straight facts.
Direct opinion (interviews with people involved).
Indirect opinion (commentators saying what they think).
Reported opinion (views reported by a commentator or presenter).

• Now consider your reaction to the story. Did you:

Understand all the facts?
Agree or disagree with the opinions?
Feel that it raised more questions than it answered?
Feel that the story was reported in a full and unbiased way?

Research B

• Now look at a range of daily newspapers, asking yourselves the same questions but substituting 'space' for 'time'.
Did you come up with the same answers? If not, why not?

Research C

• Try to find out how a TV or radio news programme, or a newspaper, is produced, and who is responsible for what is produced.

Presentation

• REPORT your conclusions and opinions (backed up by evidence) on the topic of 'Truth and the Media':

Orally to your group or class.
As a newspaper or magazine article.
As a radio talk or a Channel 4 'Comment' programme.
As a discursive essay for your classwork folio.

• Write the script of a news programme for your Local Radio.

• Compile the front page of a newspaper which will be read by other students.

• Try out the simulation games 'Radio Covingham' or 'Front Page'.

Writing a critical evaluation or personal review

• After reading fiction or watching drama or film, you should ask yourself the 7 key questions:

1 *What* happens?
2 *Where* does it happen?
3 *When* does it happen?
4 *Who* was involved?
5 *Why* was it written/scripted/filmed?
6 *Which* special techniques were used?
7 *What* is my honest and considered REACTION?

When *writing* about fiction, however, it is best to organise clearly what you wish to say. Here is a structure which you could follow if you write an evaluation or review of any of the stories in this collection.

Part 1: Introduction

• Mention the title, the writer's *name*, and say briefly what the writer's main *theme* or *concern* is.

Part 2: Setting/Plot Ending

• Say where and when the events take place.
• Write a brief outline of the *action/plot*, highlighting what is most significant and leaving out less important details.
• *Discuss* the *ending*, saying whether or not you found it effective and why.
• Say whether or not the *plot* is the most important aspect of the story.

Part 3: Characters

• Write a description of the characters who play an important role in the story. Say what they are like as people, and how you reacted to them and/or the situation they were in. (Quote words/phrases/ sentences to illustrate your comments.)

Part 4: Themes

• Now discuss the *theme* or *themes* more fully, that is, say what you think the writer's *purpose* was in writing the story. What was he/she really trying to make you aware of and think about?
• Say *how* the writer has developed or illuminated the theme(s). Was it revealed:

Through the plot?

Through the situation which the characters were in?
Through description or dialogue?
Through the use of a symbol — an object which is often referred to throughout the story, or one which is clearly important?
Through the ending of the story?

Part 5: The Writer's Craft

• Now comment on any features of the writer's craft which seemed to you to be particularly interesting, and say *why* these are effective in this story. For example, think about:

Who tells (narrates) the story; the writer or a special character who is caught up in the events?

How the plot has been structured: are there shifts of time? Where does the *climax* occur?

Is *description* and *dialogue* balanced, or if one dominates the other, why should this be so?

How the writer creates the *mood* and the *atmosphere*: e.g. conflict, tension, violence, mystery, sadness, sympathy, humour, tenderness and so on.

The writer's *style*:

Is the dialogue realistic?

Does the description make you really *see* what's being described? If it does, is this because the writer has used *similes* or *metaphors* to make a scene more vivid in your mind? Or has he/she used unusual words or combinations of words? (Quote some examples.)

Is the writing *economical* or *verbose* (long-winded). Look again at the length of the sentences and paragraphs. Short sentences may help to create pace, movement and tension. Long sentences can build up mood and atmosphere.

Part 6: Personal Response

• Finally, write your own personal, considered reaction to the story.

Did you enjoy it? Why?

How did you feel during and after reading it?

Did you find the theme, or any other aspect, particularly interesting? Why?

Did you learn anything from having read it? Are you now more aware of some aspect of your life? If so, what? (Note: It is possible to find a story, novel, or play, or film, or painting interesting but not enjoyable!)

A story will bring to you someone else's experience. What experience of life did you bring to the story?

CREATIVE WRITING

Guidelines for your coursework folio (folder).

● Read 'Kreativ Riting' by Brian McCabe, then in small groups discuss:

1   Your reactions to the story
2   What you think of Mr Pitcairn's approach to creative writing
3   Your reaction to Joe Murdoch's "Kreative, automatic, deep-sea meditating writing"
4   Why do you think he wants it to be destroyed? Do you think it should be destroyed?
5   What *is* creative writing? Can it be learned/taught? Where *does* inspiration come from?

   (You may wish to read the personal reflections of the three writers printed in this collection)

● Writing may not be a solitary activity — it's about *sharing* experiences with someone else, and *shaping* experiences (your own and others') into a pattern or *form* which will interest, entertain and intrigue the reader. Inspiration can come from:

   An *image* from life or art or a photograph
   A *person*: real or fictional
   A *situation* from your own experience or someone else's
   anger/concern: an issue which you feel strongly about
   other writers – or artists, film directors or musicians
   The *delight* of giving pleasure to others and being able to open their eyes, or the power to manipulate them

On your own

● Read the stories which follow later. These were written by students, not professional writers. *Select* the story which you think is most effective, then:

In groups

   defend your choice, listen to others and try to reach agreement
   decide whether, and how, one or all of these stories could have been improved.

On your own

● Attempt your own creative writing. Think about the stories you've just discussed and about *one* of these topics:

'Tracks' is a fantasy based on a central *image*. Try to develop one of the following into a central image for a possible story: a train, a dual carriageway, a coat, waves, a gun, a tree. Now plan and draft the story.

'The Web' creates a *person* in extreme circumstances, yet her feelings are *suggested* through a clear description of objects rather than *narrated directly*. Try to build up a story in the same way, perhaps focusing on someone who is in *despair* or *danger*; eg: after a relationship has been broken, during a kidnap, before an operation.

'The Red Scarf' develops a particular *situation*. Try to list a number of situations which could involve conflict. It's best to start from personal experience or from what you've actually heard. Newspapers deal in "story" situations. Try to find an unusual one but remember that the danger in seeking situations from the media is that your story may be derivative — second-hand. Select and develop *one* of your situations into a story. Build up the atmosphere of conflict, create realistic characters and plan for an interesting ending.

'Changes', 'A Fairy Story' and 'Colours' clearly reveal issues such as injustice, racism, bigotry and selfishness. This is done by:

   Concentrating on a single incident
   Re-writing a well known tale for a modern audience
   Developing a relationship

• List a number of issues about which you have strong feelings, then select one and try to plan the best way to dramatise it in your own story.

• Try writing an alternative version of a tale or myth for a modern audience – eg: Jack and the Beanstalk, Red Riding Hood, The Goose and the Golden Eggs.

• Take a modern myth or superhero and alter it/him/her for the purpose of humour — to entertain your reader. Here's an example, an extract from a story featuring James Bond, 007, now old and unemployed:

'Bond,' soothed Q, 'you must remember that Bilton can occasionally get quite rough. The dregs of society live here. They share toilet paper and read '*The Sun*'. They are a desperate race. They would kill for chips and pickles, and God knows, on our pay, we can't afford a loss like that. They are savages, Bond, savages. Each tribe has its own brutal way of killing... for most it's cannibalism of one form or another.' Bond listened, dumbfounded, and rubbed his aching varicose veins. Even his glass eye was steaming up. Q continued ... 'I would go myself Bond, but you can probably tell that I've put on a pound or ten so I'm not in peak condition.'

'And anyway,' concluded Q, 'you are dispensable.' For the second time, Bond found himself having an in-depth conversation with the floor-boards. Q bounced to the door, opened it and said, 'You will consider, Bond,' and gestured that it was time for Bond to leave. The agent crawled to the door and out into the cold and hostile hallway with his teeth clicking in his pocket, dragging his walking frame behind him.

Tracks

The tracks were a pair of black lines which bisected reality. In between, where the trains ran, the causeway of hardpacked earth was an area where the boundaries of normality were pushed to an extreme. On either side grew yellow blades of grass, bleached by the sun, which could offer a soft pillow for sleep or be a series of sharp knives. Today, and on every other day, the sun was a fiery orb in the sky which, like the grass, was a double-edged sword, issuing drought and warmth simultaneously. It shimmered in the azure sky.

Tracks, grass, sun, sky: this was the landscape. There were no redeeming features to be seen even on the horizon where land was welded to sky in a hazy green band. The situation was almost completely unchanging.

Why this day, out of thousands of others, was chosen is simple. On this particular day, an anomaly in the routine was encountered, this anomaly being a man.

His image wavered slightly in the heat as he emerged from the murky distance. Matted to his scalp, his hair glistened in the sticky sunshine. He wore a baggy suit which had turned brown with the accumulation of dirt, and on his head sagged a hat which had long lost its shape. Slung over his shoulder was a carpetbag as used by eloping couples in old films. Within the confines of this faded shell of fabric were all the man's possessions consisting of food, water and a few well-thumbed paperback novels.

As he ambled along the tracks, his stomach rumbled. Relays in his brain snapped impatiently telling him that food was required. He composed a meal of a mugful of gritty water and a hard, black piece of bread — completely uninspiring. Nevertheless, this was wolfed down in a matter of seconds and the man stretched out between the rails and belched contentedly.

While he watched a cloud progress across the sky and its shadow zoom across the sea of grass, his mind drifted through time to his past life. Now, he could not recall much: the monotony of years of walking had eroded his memory like rocks into sand. Much of his mind had been converted into desert but still enough remained to form a recognisable portrait of his personality.

He remembered holding the gun against his head and pulling the trigger. Then there was darkness for an indeterminable period of time. And now this: walking down the rails ever onward. When the gun fired he sought oblivion and here on an earth of the future or past or perhaps a completely different world, he had found it.

However, even in oblivion purpose existed. The tracks. Ever since he had wakened naked upon this world, a pile of clothes and a carpet bag beside him, he had been intrigued by the mystery of the railway. A railway needs trains, but where were they? He had never seen any, although many times he had awakened to the distinctive hooting noise of the whistle. Whether imagination or an actual train he could not tell.

Sounds shatter reveries.

At this instant a faint high-pitched whistle demanded an immediate response. The man stood up and surveyed his surroundings. Nothing. His armpits prickled and sweat rolled down his sides. Again, he looked. This time something could be seen. Accompanied by another whistle, out of the green horizon came a silvery blob. A warm breeze was kicked up and the grass began to ripple, gently at first but the wind increased in intensity it whipped back and forth in a raging fury.

The blob was now larger and was unmistakably a train, in that it had wheels which kept it to the tracks. Otherwise, there was nothing 'train'ish about it. No smokestacks, buffers or green paint — only a mass of complex machinery enclosed in a shell of an unknown hard, resistant alloy with exquisite curves giving it an impression of high speed even when standing still. It coasted silently for a while and rolled to a stop a few feet in front of the man.

Almost crying with relief, the man climbed aboard, discarding his belongings on the railwayside. Now he did not need to know the purpose of the tracks or the trains: this was far more important. No longer did he need to wander aimlessly along the railway.

The train which travelled the rails of this world now had a driver!

The Web

The spider fell lightly on golden spun silk, its delicate legs grasping the spindly threads. The web stretched from the petals of a rose to the grey harled wall of the cottage. The sun hung heavily in the evening sky which was empty but for a few pink-tinged drifting clouds. The garden was a peaceful tangle of grass and flowers, a timeless whisper of green.

The door of the cottage opened, breaking the stillness and the fragile web. Margie stepped out and paused on the doorstep, breathing in the hot smell of flowers. She flicked a strand of hair from her forehead and gazed into the sun, her eyes misting over from its glare.

Steam burst in humid puffs from the chrome spout with a gradual crescendo of noise. At its peak the kettle mechanically clicked off, once more like the other kitchen appliances which sat dormant on the polished worktop. A tap was turned on, spraying frigid water into the droplet-flecked sink. The washing machine shuddered into action on its final spin. Margie half listened. Her husband's voice was merging into the anonymous murmur of machinery.

That morning she had picked some flowers. Big soft-leaved roses and violet spires of delphinium. Now they sat in a cut crystal vase on the window sill, their colours caught in a swirling reflection on the side of the fridge. Her husband stared past them into the garden.

'I'll have to mow the lawn, its looking...'

'I'll do it,' said Margie. She pulled gently at a velvet petal of delphinium, releasing it, watching the delicate flowers shake. 'I've got plenty of time while you're out at work.' She paused, looking at the grass. 'I can do it tomorrow.'

The curtains had been opened. The window caught the coldness of the sun, distorting it into harsh stabs of light. She turned over. The alarm switched on and music crackled tinnily into the room. Margie was alone. A slight depression in the pillow beside her was the only sign that anyone had been there. She got up and switched off the radio, shook the duvet, dragging her fingers through her hair.

She walked through the house, past the empty chairs and polished dining-table. In the hallway the telephone crouched, its silence a threat. The kitchen door had been left standing open. Margie went in and opened the fridge. A light flicked on, accompanied by a continuous hum. The cheese glowed garishly in the luminous yellow inside.

After breakfast, Margie loaded the washing machine, stuffing limp clothes into the claustrophobic drum. She filled the small drawer with the washing powder, spilling some of the white granules and watching them scatter on the red tiled floor. The clothes churned in the soapy machine as she washed the kitchen windows, shifting aside the crystal vase. A violet flower drooped slightly, the edge of its pletals curling, staining a deep blue-black.

The washing machine coughed and groaned to a halt. The clothes sloshed from side to side, slowing to a stop in the white, foaming water. Margie stopped wiping the windows, puzzled. She dropped her cloth and went over to the machine. Crouching in front of it, the reflection of her face stretched hideously in the round glass door, she turned the knob, resetting the programme. Nothing happened, it stared back at her, mute. She banged the front with her fist and pressed the door-release button. Still nothing. Frustrated, Margie pulled at the knob and grabbed the rim of the door, her fingernails digging into the rubber seal. Again she pushed the door-release and with a click the glass pane swung open, spilling froth onto the floor, the whitish water gushing from the gaping drum. Margie cried out and jammed the door shut again. Bubbles of soap floated on the dirty pool, bursting one by one. Margie, on her hands and knees, mopped up the grey puddle.

The window was open to the soft gauze of twilight air. The breeze was enough to raise gooseflesh on her arms but she did not move away or close the window. The grass was still uncut, thick and dark. Margie leant forward, pressing her forehead on the glass, its hard coolness soothing. She closed her eyes, resting on the black pane.

The withered petals of delphinium hung limply on the browning stalks. The roses had gradually shrivelled, scorched by the magnified heat of the sun through the kitchen window.

The whine of the lawn-mower echoed in the air, killing the soft chirping of a cricket. Margie pushed the machine onto the grass, wary of the pulsing electricity which vibrated in the handle. She watched the whipping blades stained with the blood of grass. She followed it as it swept through the tangle of green, tossing aside the long svelte blades and leaving them lying in bruised heaps. The noise grew in her ears, flowing and swarming until she jerked away from the mower, unplugging the socket. The whine choked off leaving an emptiness which Margie could breath. Slowly she trailed from the garden leaving the mower in the middle of the half-shorn grass.

She lifted the dead flowers from the vase, watching the thick greenish water drip from the wounded stems. She carried the flowers through to the living room. The vacuum cleaner lay sprawled in a corner. Margie layed her withered bouquet on the hearth and sat beside it, picking up the concertina-like hose at the end of which hung the greedy nozzle. She ran her hands over the tube, stretching it and watching it spring back. Experimentally, she unscrewed the nozzle and then detached the tube from the motor. The afternoon sun shone brightly on the glazed hearth-stones. Margie picked up the concertina hose. She carried it out of the house, past the lawn and tumble of roses, to the black-windowed garage.

The door opened with a screech and Margie entered the cold darkness. Her car squatted silently within the grim concrete walls.

Outside, a spider glided from one branch of a rose to another. Again the silken thread broke, its torn ends floating in the still air. Again the spider made the leap and this time the thread held. The spider sat motionless for a moment before joining another thread, and then another, until a web gradually formed.

When it was finished, the muffled murmur of the car's engine could still be heard through the garage walls.

The Red Scarf

The dormitory was long and narrow, with beds down either side. The walls were high with windows near the ceiling, these had black blinds drawn down and the room was in darkness apart from one light. A table lamp illuminated a desk at the bottom of the room.

Here sat the night nurse with her feet up on a chair and a cover over her legs to keep out the cold night draughts. She had been reading but now her eyes were closed, 'not sleeping but resting' she always said if disturbed. The residents called her 'Old Mary' and she ruled their world at night by fear. Her tongue was her weapon and with it she threatened the withdrawal of privileges, or even worse. She could make the most determined spirit submit. All she wanted was a quiet night to rest her eyes when not reading or knitting.

The thirty bodies that slept made the usual noises that human beings make when sleeping. All eyes were closed except one pair. They belonged to Frank, and Frank did not intend to sleep tonight. He had a plan.

He was not a happy man, he did not even know what "happy" meant. He understood pain, sadness and fear. Particularly fear, he lived with that every day of his life. He had problems with communication but as he had been beaten into submission as a child, he was not aggressive. This resulted in his being the victim of everyone's moods and his life was spent in an aura of constant friction.

Today had been a bad day from beginning to end. When Old Mary's shrill voice had shouted the command, 'Everyone up. Now!' he had awakened in a wet bed and the fear of the ridicule that would follow set in. He had just lain there hoping that all the men would have gone for breakfast by the time he got up. Especially Billy, for he loved a scene. This resulted in Old Mary pulling back the covers and the name calling had started. Everyone had joined in, mostly to side with Old Mary, but not Billy, he just enjoyed hurting.

By the time he had cleaned up his bed and himself and taken the wet clothes to the laundry, breakfast was finished and he had to do without.

The rest of the day was spent in the therapy room making baskets. Frank had poor co-ordination and he was not very quick at feeding the needle through the tough loops on the base of the basket. The little concentration he had was constantly disturbed by Billy, who either bumped into him just as he had the needle in the correct position or who sat grinning at him with his mouth. This made Frank's hand shake so much that he had achieved very little in the whole day, much to the therapists' irritation.

But this evening had been really bad. He had not meant to drop his plate, it had just slipped out of his hands and his supper had landed all over the floor. It had happened just as Old Mary had come on duty and it had made her so angry that she had told Billy to take him to the toilet block for punishment. Everyone had fallen silent, for they knew what was going to happen. Old Mary never hit anyone, she used Billy to give that type of punishment. And punish Frank he did, by wetting a towel and hitting him all over his body, not his face because that would have marked, and he had taken such pleasure in his actions.

It was when Frank was lying on the floor, nursing his aching body he had decided on his plan. Tonight he would run away.

He lay awake thinking over the whole day and trying to decide what to take. He had no personal possessions, only a red fluffy scarf that a kind student had given him a few months before. He liked the scarf. He kept it behind the pipes in the bathroom and every now and again he took it out and touched it. He knew if he showed it to anyone it would go missing, so it was his secret.

When he was sure Old Mary was resting her eyes he crept into the bathroom and took his scarf. He was suddenly very frightened of being caught and he climbed out of the bathroom window into the cold winter night.

The cold air hit his body and the stones hurt his feet. He had forgotten to dress and put on his shoes. He was not sure where he was going, his plan was just to go.

He walked onto the grass as his feet were sore, but soon the ice froze his feet and he felt no pain. It was two miles from the hospital to the main gate, not that Frank knew that, he just kept on walking. He followed the road clutching his red scarf and he stumbled on. He was very cold and very frightened, he was sorry that he had left his bed, he wanted to return but he thought of Old Mary and Billy and became frightened.

In the early, grey morning the mini-bus made its way from the main raod into the hospital grounds carrying the first batch of workers. The headlights caught a strange sight. Just at the gates lay a man, curled into a ball, clutching a red scarf which had frozen solid to the ground. He was dead.

Old Mary, having rested her eyes, raised her voice and shouted, 'Everyone up. Now!'

Changes

Mr McAlistair was a short man, maybe that was the reason why he pushed his pupils out of the way so roughly, why he never smiled, why he never took an interest in his pupils. He kept a barrier between himself and the rest. Mr McAlistair felt threatened: times were changing fast and with changing times came changing values. Children were treated more liberally, and as a result the layer surrounding Mr McAlistair was becoming horny and brittle.

Many of the younger staff felt he was near snapping point. They could see that his iron-like ruling over class discipline was corroding fast.

A normal day. He would start the lesson;

'Homework. Hand it in. I expect twenty-one books.'

Nobody listened — the boys called each other names from one end of the room to another, girls huddled round in small groups, giggling and occasionally glancing up at the awaiting teacher.

'Right, can we get started, page twenty-nine.'

Suddenly somebody flung a book from the back of the class. It hit the blackboard, just above Mr McAlistair's head. As he spun round the class saw his face, they sniggered as they saw him struggling for self-control: McAlistair absorbed every face looking back at him, jeering and insolent. He wanted to scream and shout at the boy. He wanted to rush to the back of the class, grab him and shake him.

'Who was that?'

The class were now in uproar: shouts from the back.

'Twas Greeny Sir. Aye Greeny'.

He looked at the boy Green. Large and muscular, a real smart alick. Green grinned back, inviting McAlistair to fight. He wanted to see him in action. Was he on form? Remember last week with Jimmy Summerville? What a laugh.

McAlistair saw this. He knew what would happen. He felt the need for control; that look haunted him. The anger within him surged up, bubbling, boiling, brimming.....

'You boy, Ali! Ali Achmed! Get up!'

He pointed to a small Asian boy at the back of the class.

'I saw you throw that book. Damn impudence, stand up straight! How dare you treat school property like this! You may bloody-well do it in Bangladesh, but you don't do it here. Do ...do you understand?'

The boy looked aghast. He stepped forward. He tried to explain; it wasn't him, he didn't throw the book...McAlistair grabbed him by the shirt collar, and raced him from the room.

He came back in and slammed the door, but this time his entrance sent a ripple of fear down many backs.

Those who wore older clothes, who took free school meals, who came from broken home families, crouched in their seats. Pushing themselves back into their chairs in fear that they fell under his gaze.

McAlistair ran his fingers through his hair as he walked back to the blackboard. He smoothed his hair back over his bald crown. Things would be all right now; in the meantime. Yes, others might allow them to carry-on in their classes, but not Mr McAlistair. He wouldn't change — never.

A Fairy Story for the 90's: The Shoemender and the Goblins

There once was a man who lived in a small town. He owned a small shop and in this shop he mended shoes. But sadly, his business was not doing very well and day after day he sat alone in his shop drinking cups of coffee and smoking cigarettes.

One day when he was closing up his shop, he felt very depressed. His shop was doing badly and he was not making any money. Soon he would be bankrupt and he would have to close up his shop for good. This thought made him very upset and, to cheer himself up, he went home and drank a hot cup of Horlicks and smoked a cigarette.

Meanwhile, back at the shop, a wondrous thing was happening. Four goblins had climbed in through a broken window and, with needle and thread, they were mending shoes. They mended all sorts; large ones, small ones, pink ones, blue ones. They worked all through the night and in the morning, as the sun was just beginning to rise, they left the shop through the broken window and went home.

When the shoemender opened the door of his shop the next morning he was astounded. There were rows of neatly mended shoes stretching from one end of the room to the other. The shoemender rubbed his eyes in disbelief and was so shocked he had to sit down for a cup of coffee and a cigarette.

After a time he began to recover and examined the shoes more closely. He bent down on his hands and knees, turned the shoes over and scrutinised them carefully. He was amazed at the size of the tiny stitches and the amount of work that had gone into each shoe. Every one was a masterpiece, a work of pure genius.

The customers obviously thought so too, for as they came, one by one, to collect their shoes they all praised the high quality of the repair. The shoemender's eyes twinkled and he beamed upon everyone who entered the shop. At the end of the day the shoemender felt happy and, as he jumped into bed, he hoped his troubles would soon be over.

That same night, the four goblins entered the shop, this time using the door, for the shoemender had left it unlocked. Again, they mended shoes all night and just before morning returned home. When the shoemender opened the shop and saw the shoes he was delighted. As the customers streamed in he knew his fortune was made. He was gaining a reputation for shoe mending and people from far and wide brought their worn and damaged shoes to be repaired in his little shop.

This went on, night after night, for six months. The goblins repaired the shoes by night and the shoemender sold them by day. Soon he was making a lot of money and became very rich.

One day the shoemender decided that he was going to expand his business in order to make more money. So he bought a larger shop and installed expensive machines which would mend shoes both quickly and efficiently. He was pleased with the result and thought of how well he was doing in life.

The goblins, however, did not realise what had happened and they turned up, as usual, to the shoemender's shop. They found the door locked and all the windows boarded up. There was no way in and so the goblins went home. Every night for a week they came to the shop and tried to get in, but realising the futility of the exercise they eventually went home.

Gradually the goblins stopped going to the shop and began to lose interest. They never went anywhere and just stayed in their house. From morning until night they did nothing and finally the goblins died.

The shoemender sat in his big shop, fat and prosperous, drinking cups of coffee and smoking cigarettes.

Colours

The autumn sun was setting over Glasgow, forming a red haze over the skyline. From a distance the city seemed dead but all the pubs were alive with people talking about "the match".

Although the sun was now almost gone it was still warm enough and light enough for children to be out playing. Between two tenements two boys were kicking a football to each other. The tenements stood almost like a sleeping body, but the heart, the two boys, still beat with life. Underneath the doorway to the back green, a dog and cat lay sleeping in the last light of the day.

'Right we'll play three an' yer in,' cried Ian, the taller of the two.

They had tied a washing line between two clothes poles. Damien crouched between them, awaiting any attempt Ian made at scoring a goal. Damien seemed the quieter boy, thin faced with a dark complexion. Both wore jeans and sweatshirts which looked to be hand-me-downs from older brothers or cousins.

Ian took his first shot. The ball headed straight for the left corner. Damien made no attempt to save it. Goal. Ian retrieved the ball and with his second shot scored again. Once more, Damien made little attempt to save. With the third ball Ian, acting smart, kicked it a few times above his head making Damien watch with amusement, then belted the spinning sphere straight between the poles. Third goal.

'You're bloody useless you. Ye'll no play for the Rangers like that. Ye gawn the game the morn?' Ian asked, smiling at his achievement. Three goals with three shots.

'Aye ma faither's takin me,' Damien replied. He seemed almost embarrassed at his feeble attempts at being a goalkeeper.

'Ma auld man says we're gonna cuff they papes.'

Damien looked confused, 'Aye. Whit are these papes? They the Rangers? Aye?'

'You ken nothin,' Ian said in a lecturing voice. He continued, 'Papes are catholics. The Celtic ken. Naebody likes papes, so ma faither says.'

'A support the Celtic an' am a catholic,' Damien replied quietly, almost hoping his friend would not hear him.

'My God! Ah, Ah mean, goodness me,' Ian gasped, almost shocked — a little ashamed.

'Is that the time? A better get ma tea.'

Ian picked up the ball and ran towards his door, where the dog and cat snuggled together peacefully. Damien walked off in the other direction. As Ian passed the animals he stamped his foot, the noise echoed through the quiet stair. The cat jumped to its feet, startling its companion, who then chased it, teeth bared.

The next day Glasgow was a mass of colour. Green and blue. Crowds of youths began to gather on street corners, all green or all blue: apart.

Ian watched from the bedroom window of his tenement flat as Damien appeared from the doorway with his father, sporting a large green rosette. He had a green and white scarf covered in badges around his neck and a green tammy carrying a Celtic patch. Overnight Ian had grown to hate his friend.

'Look at him,' he thought, 'People'll think 'ese a bloody hedge wi' aw that green on.'

Damien and his father merged with an impatient group, and the green and white mob moved off down the street.

It was Ian's turn to go now. Every item of clothing he wore had

'Rangers' stamped somewhere. His father led him out of the tenement as a crowd of Celtic supporters passed. He shielded his son from them, almost as if they were evil. They crossed the road to where their own kind could be found, the blue; ranked on one side of the street. Green massed on the other.

Crowds formed at the turnstiles, green and blue, now mingling. Tension was growing and the faces of the policemen looked anxious.

'A didnae ken yer friend wiz a wee pape,' Ian's father said to his son. He had spotted him in the crowd. Ian pretended not to hear but his father repeated his statement, this time louder. Ian just said 'aye.'

The gates opened and the crowd began to surge forward like light bursting into a room when curtains are opened in the morning.

'Every man fur himsell,' was shouted from the mass. Both Ian's and Damien's fathers got the boot in. The two boys glanced at each other. When their eyes met they both quickly looked away, embarrassed.

An army of policemen arrived. 'Quick it's the polis.' The fight was over before it really started. All but the few who managed to run away were bundled into the awaiting Black Marias.

The two boys stood alone, each one silently blaming the other for what had happened.

'You boys better get hame, eh,' said a policeman.

The boys walked off together, neither wishing to make the first move in any conversation.

'Whit did yer faither go an' day that fur?' Ian said angrily.

'It wisnae ma faither, it wiz yours,' Damien said protectively. He continued, 'Look maybe baith wir at fault. Or maybe neither. A thought we wir pals, anyway.'

'Aye,' Ian replied quietly.

The two turned into the street and arrived at the open tenement doorway. The cat and the dog lay asleep, once more side by side, both content, each sharing the warmth of the other.

'Fancy a game o' fitba after yer tea?'

'Aye, Rangers and Celtic?'

'Naw.'

*F*urther Reading

Bernard MacLaverty

Secrets and other stories, Blackstaff Press
A Time to Dance and other stories, Penguin
The Great Profundo and other stories, Cape
Cal, Penguin
Lamb, Penguin

Brian McCabe

The Lipstick Circus (stories), Mainstream
Spring's Witch (poetry), Mariscat Press
One Atom to Another (poetry), Polygon

George Mackay Brown

Andrina (stories), The Hogarth Press
Hawkfall (stories), The Hogarth Press
A Time to Keep (stories), The Hogarth Press
A Calendar of Love (stories), The Hogarth Press
Greenvoe (a novel), The Hogarth Press
Magnus (a novel), The Hogarth Press
Selected Poems, The Hogarth Press
Orkney Tapestry (non-fiction), Quartet

Joan Lingard

The Prevailing Wind, Paul Harris
Sisters by Rite, Hamish Hamilton
Reasonable Doubts, Pan
The Sadie and Kevin Quintet, Puffin
The Maggie Quartet, Beaver
Snake Among the Sunflowers, Canongate Kelpie
The Winter Visitor, Puffin

*A*cknowledgements

The editor and publishers would like to express thanks to the following for permission to reproduce personal essays and stories in this collection:

Brian McCabe, George Mackay Brown, and Dilys Rose, for their personal essays, contributed specially for this collection.

'Silver Linings' © Joan Lingard: David Higham Associates.

'A Time to Dance' © Bernard MacLaverty: Jonathan Cape Ltd. Originally published in anthology of same name.

'Anima' and 'The Full Moon' © Brian McCabe: Mainstream Publishing Ltd.

'Secrets' © Bernard MacLaverty: Blackstaff Press Ltd.

'Silver', 'The Wireless Set' and 'Andrina' © George Mackay Brown: The Hogarth Press.

'Remote' © Bernard MacLaverty: Jonathan Cape Ltd. Originally published in *The Great Profundo*.

'A House on Christmas Hill' © Wilma Murray: Association for Scottish Literary Studies, first published in New Writing Scotland.

'Magnolia', 'Snakes and Ladders', 'I Can Sing, Dance, Rollerskate', © Dilys Rose, 1987; 1985; 1986. 'Magnolia' and 'Snakes and Ladders' were first published in the magazine *Radical Scotland*; 'I Can Sing, Dance, Rollerskate', first broadcast on BBC Radio 3.

'The Hunter of Dryburn' © Brian McCabe: Mainstream Publishing Limited.

'Kreativ Riting' © Brian McCabe: Collins Publishers. Originally published in *I Can Sing, Dance, Rollerskate and Other Stories by Scottish Writers*.

Unwin Hyman English Series

Series editor: Roy Blatchford
Advisers: Jane Leggett and Gervase Phinn

Unwin Hyman Short Stories

Openings   edited by Roy Blatchford
Round Two   edited by Roy Blatchford
School's OK   edited by Josie Karavasil and Roy Blatchford
Stepping Out   edited by Jane Leggett
That'll Be The Day   edited by Roy Blatchford
Sweet and Sour   edited by Gervase Phinn
It's Now or Never   edited by Jane Leggett and Roy Blatchford
Pigs Is Pigs   edited by Trevor Millum
Dreams and Resolutions   edited by Roy Blatchford

Unwin Hyman Collections

Free As I Know   edited by Beverley Naidoo
Solid Ground   edited by Jane Leggett and Sue Libovitch
In Our Image   edited by Andrew Goodwyn

Unwin Hyman Plays
Stage Write   edited by Gervase Phinn